Jan J. Dominique

❧ *Memoir of an Amnesiac* ❧

Translated by Irline François

Title: Memoir of an Amnesiac
Author: Jan J. Dominique
Cover Collage by Ralph Allen
Cover and Layout design: Nathalie Jn Baptiste
© Copyright 2008, Caribbean Studies Press
Coconut Creek, FL

Published in French as *Mémoire d'une amnésique,* by Jan
J. Dominique, Montréal: Les Éditions du CIDIHCA,
2004.

For information, please contact:

Caribbean Studies Press
7550 NW 47th Avenue
Coconut Creek, FL 33073
Telephone: 954-968-7433
Fax: 954-970-0330
E-mail: caribbeanstudiespress@earthlink.net
Web: www.caribbeanstudiespress.com

ISBN 13: 987-1-58432-473-7
ISBN 10: 1-58432-473-2

Table of Contents

Acknowledgments

I have carried this book with me in so many bags and to so many places since I bought it in 1988 at the *Librairie Générale* in Pointe-à-Pitre, Guadeloupe that in no way can I measure the debts accumulated along the way.

Time is not the only reason I cannot retrace all my debts: this book stands at the junction of emotive, intellectual communities that it straddles and unites without closure. My heartfelt thanks to Jeff François for his unswerving support, love, and steadfastness in helping me sustain my enthusiasm for this novel; Solange François for her boundless wit and strength, shrewdly cultivating my linguistic, interpreting and translating skills in my multiple languages; Fabienne François whose deft ear, meticulous and discerning eye took me through this manuscript to its final form; Jerry François for preserving the memories of our childhood alive.

I owe special thanks to a number of friends whose comments and careful readings or editing were both a challenge and an inspiration: Marie-Josèphe Silver for her friendship, patience and generous assistance on various parts of the book, sharing with me the delights, frustrations, pain and exquisite pleasure in finding *le mot juste*; Jennifer Bess, for her patience, whose insights combine a critical eye, sharp advice and unbridled enthusiasm. To my marvelous women accomplices and confidantes: Marjorie Attignol

Salvodon, Carmen Oquendo-Villar, Emily Dalgarno, Johanna Garvey, Lucrèce Louishon-Louinis, Pina Belperio and Brigitte Marti, a profound debt of gratitude for filling my life with love, laughter, lots of *Malbec* wine, sociopolitical insight and intellectual brilliance. To Marie-Agnès Sourieau, Micheline Rice-Maximin and Brinda Mehta, I thank for their support and encouragement in trusting this project from the very beginning.

I thank the staff and faculty of Women's Studies, English, Modern Languages, Political Science, Philosophy and Religion at Goucher College especially Marianne Githens, Steven De Caroli, Kelly Brown Douglas, Madison Smartt Bell, Michelle Tokarczyk, Seble Dawit and Gail Edmonds for their insightful comments, and support as I presented segments of this text at my post-sabbatical presentation. Thank you to President Sanford Ungar and Dean Michael Curry who supported my sabbatical semester leave enabling me to devote myself to this book. I owe more to my (former) students in women's studies, literature classes as well as other classes than they will ever know, especially Kai Hirano, Jennifer Ellsworth, Rebecca Garonzik, Alexis Iammarino, Katherine McAllister and Alyse Campbell.

I warmly thank Jan Dominique for her humor,

generosity, the strength of her words, her affirmation of the beauty and perspicacity of our Haitian *récits*. Her words have nourished, illuminated and guided me throughout this lengthy and onerous project. Carol Hollander at Caribbean Studies Press is an exemplary editor whose dedication to this text and valuable comments on the drafts carried through this project to fruition; to Edwidge Danticat for her wonderful preface to this work. *Merci de tout coeur.*

This book is dedicated to the memory of both my father Gérard François and my staunch ally/friend Gay Wilentz. I grieve over the losses of the two people whose wisdom, nurturing, love and passion for knowledge, justice and life has sustained and guided my own. Both during their lifetimes and from beyond the grave, they have influenced this project in ways that are transparent and intricate. My debt to them cannot be measured.

Foreword

I first read J. J. Dominique's *Mémoire d'une Amnésique* in 1986 when I could still read an entire book in French without referring to a dictionary. I had left Haiti five years before at age twelve and had moved, or had been moved, to the United States to be reunited with my parents who'd left before me, in search of an economically and politically improved life. Upon their arrival in the United States, my parents did find a life that was "better" on those terms, but the cost to them was great. They worked around the clock, sometimes even while seriously ill, and could not even consider themselves "free" because, being undocumented for many years, they were always looking over their shoulders. Freedom came when my two American brothers were born in Brooklyn and my parents were, after nearly a decade, able to get their papers and send for my brother Bob and me. Freedom for them, but not for me and Bob, who were just starting the vicious cycle our parents had entered as migrants before us, discovering for ourselves what it was like to understand nothing of what was said outside of your house.

This feeling of being stranded led our parents to read, which was a good example for us in terms of seeking solace from a book. While my parents exclusively read the bible, I enjoyed the kinds of earthly stories my migration had severed me from, the porch narratives of my childhood in which I could completely recognize myself. Being relatively new to a place where I had little history, but where my new schoolmates felt free to call me dirty Haitian, Frenchie or boat people, I hungered for words from home. Reading here would not be like reading back in Haiti. Here I needed words to remember and recreate myself. In the Haiti that I had left behind, where rote memorization was the primary method of learning for all school-age children and young adults, I had memorized and then had quickly forgotten at least a million words, but I had never savored them. If anything I had resented them, their length, their impenetrability, their irrelevance to my tropical reality. We had, for example, to memorize lessons about seasons, which listed them as spring, summer, winter, and fall, without acknowledging the dry and rainy cycles around us. At least we were not obliged to say "Our ancestors the Gauls," with our African lips while staring ahead from our black faces with our dark eyes. But there were still erasures that were just as grave, one of them being the fact that no one I knew in my age group had ever been given a novel written by a Haitian writer to read. What we did get were French novels, *Camille and The Three Musqueteers* among them, which are perhaps Haitian novels because Alexandre Dumas father and son had a Haitian grandmother and great-grandmother in Marie-Cesette

Dumas.

We also read the meticulous details of Emile Zola's downtrodden classes, which did echo some of the realities of the impoverished ghetto where I grew up. These and the fables of Jean de La Fontaine, the *pensées* of Blaise Pascal and the crude jokes of François Rabelais filled whatever space and time might have been devoted to homegrown contemporary talent. My young female literature teacher in primary school loved French literature so much that she was always quoting from it. "As the writer said," she would begin every sentence, never bothering to identify the writer, but later I would realize that she'd been citing Voltaire, Racine, and Baudelaire, writers whose words she thought we could not be fully "civilized" without having been exposed to. If she knew of the existence of Haitian writers, she never betrayed the fact. I don't know why neither she nor the Haitian education department, which could have made it mandatory, did not want us to read our own authors. However, during my twelve years in Haiti, I never knew that writers like J. J Dominique existed or could exist.

I first read J. J. Dominique's Mémoire d'une Amnésique in 1986 when I could still read an entire book in French without referring to a dictionary. At fifteen, after having lived in the United States for a while, I went in search of reading material at the main branch of Brooklyn Public Library one Saturday afternoon and was shocked to come across two new and narrow shelves of books labeled Livres Haitiens or Haitian books. The thirty-year Duvalier dictatorship had just ended in Haiti and perhaps the Haitian patrons of the Brooklyn library had demanded books about themselves, to help them interpret their ever-changing country from afar.

The day I discovered the small Haitian books section, I checked out the only two remaining novels among the poetry collections and political essays: J.J. Dominique's *Mémoire* and Jacques Roumain's *Gouverneurs de la Rosée*. Because it was shorter, I devoured the Roumain first and perhaps it is thanks to that first eager reading that I have tried to maintain a silent conversation with Roumain that publically manifested itself in the title of my 2004 novel in stories *The Dew Breaker*, a book which I neither intended to be a novel nor a story collection, but something in between. The longing to speak back to Roumain is not mine alone. In a written tribute on the hundredth anniversary of his birth, J.J. Dominique wrote:

> Au fil des années, Jacques Roumain a souvent été present dans ma vie. Pour des raisons diverses, allant de la littérature à la politique, du vodou aux choix linguistiques, de considé-

rations personelles à des activités professionel-
les. Roumain a, par moments, accompagné
mon quotidien de journaliste, d'enseignante,
de citoyenne et, surtout, j'ai ressenti son
absence, dans ma conscience d'orpheline littéraire.

[Over the years, Jacques Roumain has often
been present in my life. For various reasons,
ranging from literature to politics, to vodou,
to linguistic choices, to personal considera-
tions and professional activities. Roumain has
sometimes infiltrated my daily life as a journalist, teacher, citizen, and most of all, I have
felt his absence in my awareness of being a literary orphan.]

In as much as our stories are the bastard children
of everything we've ever experienced and read, my
desire to tell an ambiguous story, in a collaged manner, to merge into my narrative the oral narratives of
my childhood, probably begins with my reading of
the book you are about to read, a book which could
have only been written by a literary orphan to offer,
among other things, a hybrid literary heritage to
other literary orphans.

Maxims about judging a book by its cover aside,

when I first picked up the novel, I was of course drawn to its paradoxical title. How can an amnesic remember? Perhaps there is a special kind of memory allowed to amnesiacs. One that only other amnesiacs share. I had grown up steeped in orality but I had never seen it written down before, especially in such an intricate and graceful way. Here was an insightful and nuanced examination of a complex father/daughter relationship, a deeply moving exploration of childhood, complicated by a brutal dictator who to his arsenal of psychological weapons, adds folktales, turning old myths into living nightmares. Thus the legend of the Tonton Macoutes, bogeymen who come to take naughty children away in a knapsack, becomes a real life militia of denim clad killers, henchmen and women who would assassinate their own mothers and fathers if so ordered by the dictator. A foreign journalist once asked François "Papa Doc" Duvalier what he represented for Haitians and Duvalier replied that he was their father and the Virgin Mary their mother. He also dressed as the guardian of the cemetery, the Baron Samedi, a symbol of death. Thus we were all meant to be like the young Pauls, both daughter and father, terrified children who could not even be sure who to look in the eye or smile at or love. For love could too easily turn into something ugly, something that can only be expressed through violence. A slap that protects from greater injuries. Coldness that hides a fear of attachment. Because who knows when we might have to leave? Who knows when we might have to die? Who knows if we are worth remembering once we perish?

Grappling with memory is, I believe, a Haitian obsession. We have, it seems, a collective agreement as Haitians to remember our triumphs and gloss over our failures. Thus we speak of the Haitian revolution as though it had just happened yesterday while we rarely speak of the slavery, which prompted it. Our paintings show glorious Eden-like African jungles yet never the middle passage. At times we cultivate communal and historical amnesia, continually repeating cycles that we never see coming until we relive the same horrors.

Never again will foreigners trample Haitian soil, the founders of the republic declared in 1804. Yet in 1915, the "boots" invaded assuring that the narrator's father will never truly know a fully free and sovereign life, having had not just his country but his imagination invaded and occupied, by the Americans, the so called boots, whose presence is used to frighten him into drinking his milk.

Pondering all this, I have read the novel several times all the while imagining the writer/narrator constantly constructing and revising her pages. In her story, I found echoes of my own. My grandfather had been a Caco, a freedom fighter against the 1915-1934 U.S. occupation and my own father had disappeared to New York when I was two and had suddenly returned for a brief visit to Haiti when I was seven, my father also an appealing stranger whose beard tickled my face in a way that both fascinated and irked me. I too had a grandmother who had died in our house and whose corpse I had watched over for a few hours before she was transported to a morgue. I knew a girl who forgot that she'd been told to say that her uncle wasn't home when the Tonton Macoutes came looking for him and because she had been unable to lie caused her uncle's death. She was ten years old and was haunted by this until she died later that same year, crushed under the wheel of a car, while walking to school.

"Her head had been in the clouds ever since she gave her uncle away," the neighbors said. Could she at ten have already known as Albert Camus wrote that there is but one true philosophical problem and that is suicide. Later I would struggle to recall the exact dates and times of these events and would doubt in my own mind whether they even took place at all.

There are many ways that our mind protects us from present and past horrors. One way is by allowing us to forget. Forgetting is a constant fear in any writer's life. In migration, far from home, memory becomes an even deeper scar. It is as if we had been forced to step under the notorious forgetting trees (the sabliyes) that our slave ancestors were told would remove their past from their heads. We know we must pass under the tree, but we hold our breaths and cross our fingers and toes and hope the forgetting wind will not fully penetrate our brains.

But what happens when we cannot tell our own stories, when our memory/ies has/have completely abandoned us? What's left is longing for something we are not even sure we ever had, but are certain we will never experience again.

"I love memories," the struggling writer/narrator declares, "on glossy paper.... One never desperately catches sadness in snapshots but the smiles at times look like grimaces." Memory that when not frozen in time is excruciating, yet she has no choice but to write through these agonies because, for one, the books she loves are forbidden. Their mere presence in her house can possibly result in someone's arrest or death. In order to read, she must also write.

How does anyone write neat, happy linear stories after having lived all this? How can we not write in codes when many of those who came before us lost their lives because they thought they had nothing to hide? This book refuses simplification. It also refuses to be reductive about love, family, memory, and about Haiti. The narrator's father tells her that she is supposed to write for all those who come after her. And she does. She writes for her unborn child, for friends and lovers, for the living and the dead and she writes for herself.

"Writing is the enemy of forgetfulness," the British novelist Anita Brookner once said. "For the writer, there is no oblivion." We are lucky that both J.J. Dominique and Paul have conquered oblivion and told their stories.

"The text is the axis," they write. Go towards the axis now. There is much to discover there.

Edwidge Danticat
January 2008

ONE

The Little Boy

July 28, 1915, the marines land to "protect the life and property of the foreigners"; The Americans had taken over Port au Prince and were occupying the Republic of Haiti. They will stay nineteen years. Among their achievements: setting up a telephone network, bringing electricity to certain areas, demobilizing the peasant masses, tarring numerous roads, creating and training the national police force, assassinating the Caco chiefs after disbanding the insurgent peasants, inaugurating schools, purging the administration of *L'Hôpital Général,* and the panic fear of a little boy who did not want to drink his milk.

In this country as probably in many others, adults proud of their physical superiority often show it by frightening children. Most are not aware of this abuse of power, absolutely convinced are they to provide the child with useful taboos for his development and his adaptation to social life. All this preamble to explain that if the parents of little Paul or Paulo used to scare him, it was with the very best of intentions.

The little boy did not like milk. They needed to have the patience of a saint to get him to drink it and it was not every day that the busy parents could spend a relatively long time persuading the little boy. Sometimes, they lost their patience and dealt with the most urgent thing first: "If you do not drink your milk, Santa will not come!" But, at Christmas, they themselves forgot and showed no difference whatso-ever between the respective merits of their thirteen children. Besides, Santa Claus was supposed to be so sensible! A worried Paulo would find his tiny gift among the others, at the foot of the scrawny tree, and the threat of Santa Claus lost all its effectiveness. And it was thus with all the bogeymen and punishments they came up with for the health of the child.

Until one day when... in a flash, an epiphany! It was all at once something audacious, a hope, a con-fession, a scream and the first lesson. And the child, born thirteen years later, could not imagine the incredible changes. This bogeyman, he was there, oppressive, intrusive and so visible.

On the balcony of the green house, when he saw them, helmets and boots on, walking down the little street, paralyzed by fear, he would scream: "No! no!" and in a quavering voice he would end up by promising: "Americans, Americans, I am going to drink my milk! Do not hurt me, American, I will be good!"

He will be six years old when they leave but the impression will remain. I remember the sentence that is part of the stories told in the evenings: he was six years old when they left and for me that date marks our birth into this world, those six years hav-ing been enough to build up our rage and constitute

our heritage. They, their presence, a logical conse-
quence of promises 'gone astray' of the great
upheaval. For them, it was also the opportunity of a
new upheaval which will not take place.

Why choose the infamous mark of their presence to begin her tale of hatred? She could have chosen any other time, any other symbol, any other out-
rage. But there is the little boy who did not want to
drink his milk. But there was their physical presence,
an insult to the memory; lucidly searching for some
positive signs of the great upheaval. But the shame
was there, not for having suffered the affront and put
up with the arrogance, but for squatting, without
moving, on the remnants of our heritage, for not all
rising together and recovering the memories of the
stormy nights, for abandoning those alone who had
not forgotten. But there was this woman who refused
a reassuring simplification. It was necessary to begin
the story, so why not with the terror shining in the
eyes of the little boy. He was not there when they
came, he will be too young when they left, for they
came quietly and went away one morning, with their
nonchalant gait.

*The first to have seen them. Who was the first? The
one who received the first slap? They should have known,
or at least foreseen the end, to worry about that person.
Leaving her house? Or rather strolling down the street,*

23

looking at the interiors of stores not knowing that no one would remember the first day. What was she thinking of? What went on in her head, in her heart? What happened to her body in front of all these foreign beings? She closes her eyes, opens them; was she blind? Her ears perceive the sound of footsteps, this dull sound of boots on the beaten path. She tries to count. One, twenty-five, ten thousand. What does it matter? They are here. Within earshot, the sound gets closer. Motionless, she senses their approach. She wants to run away. But where? The boots walk past her without noticing the presence of the only witness. Anonymous. The boots could care less about this lone blind person, petrified at the corner of a street. The boots could care less about this country. The boots know nothing. They have been sent, they have been given orders, they have embarked on gigantic boats. The boots have left their wives and children behind. Perhaps the boots felt like crying. No pity for the boots. One must not feel sorry for them. One must remember everything, all of it. For the blind man, they will remain the boots of the first day. Later on, he will no longer hear the sound of the footsteps. His ears will fill up with the noise of guns and shots. Later on, he will understand that his ears had not fooled him. These boots on the damp soil (was it raining that day?), the boots were the Other. Maybe on that very same day, did the boots become canons and guns? It is only necessary to determine the exact moment the blind man became aware of the change. At the moment when faking a smile was no longer needed? The day when what had been for so long took place.

And yet, they do not interest me. They are without a doubt too close, too present in time, too heavy on my memory. Those who lived squatting on their heels no longer fascinate me, I leave their remains to the specialists. I choose the others for the proximity, the memory still alive in so many bodies, for the presence still real under another face, for the violence of the dreams. Obsessive presence in a still blurred future; women do not have a sense of history. Bitter laughs. Above all, women do not make sense in history, they are only good for... if you do not drink your milk, I am calling the American.

I have just made up my mind. Coming home from work, I did not feel like cooking, reading, or going out again, and I know what this lack of desire means.

I have thought for a while about my escape of these last three days, about my conversation with Martine telling her how fed up I am, about the letters to Steve, and especially about Paul's visit. I was not satisfied with the text. I feel I must write it, finish it, but it's a total blank. I need to write this book. I remember explaining to Eli the two poles of interest in my life, and his teasing: the Country is the abscissa, the Text is the axis. I am a curve which at times moves up, at times moves down; I have not thought of an order of importance, they are linked; it cannot be otherwise. Both are so intimately linked that I am beginning to reflect on the meaning of the emptiness I feel. I feel like destroying the pages already written, I am not satisfied with them, they do not convey what I feel, think, live. When I write, there is between my head and my hand a distance that distorts everything, that masks my true being. Paul has read my text and spoken of a gag. Yes, I am gagged: I gag myself; I would like to, I want to remove this gag but it is holding on tightly, I feel it ensnaring my fingers the same way it often stops my mouth. I find it so difficult to tell others what I really feel, perhaps out of a fear to reveal myself, to lay myself bare, or because I have not learned how. I do not believe so. I do not want to.

I am fleeing. For weeks I have been dreading so much my moments of solitude with the text that I make them impossible. And when my desire is too strong, I reread some pages, correcting a word, a sentence, while still not liking the whole. I have dragged the text along with me everywhere, with a few blank pages which have remained just so. I was comfortable with them, my friends, my new loves, but in the background this impression of fleeing that spoiled everything, that even poisoned my love for Eli. I felt like I was giving him moments I was stealing from the text. I feel this more and more often and I am going to end up not being able to stand us. I will end up hating these others whose intrusions I usual-

ly allow with pleasure, or I will destroy the text and my need to write. Tearing up these pages will be much easier than stopping the churning, in my head, of all these stories which I am not able to convey the way I understand them, see them, because I see and hear them in my head. They are here, somewhere, ready to be transcribed. I have noted in a letter to Steve that I had the feeling of not being able to write because I did not know how and of running away, of finding excuses in order to hide this inability. Nothing is forcing you to, he answered, if you want to write, that's your right. It will be up to me to refuse to be the reader of your absurdities. His light tone had done me good. I have the right to do it, I am gagged neither by the gesture nor by the words. Despite my doubt and anguish, I write now without any constraint, in order to talk to myself: I write now the stories I hear in my head without any restraint. I have no fear, I can tell it all. The gag is my fear, what the words can reveal, what they can say without my permission. I want so much to control them, to sift them, that they are losing the life I would like to breathe into them: impoverished, sterilized, they become hollow, empty, as empty as these days of fleeing. I do not know how to write this story that I keep telling myself all day long and everyday; I do not find the way to break and destroy my fear. Paul has told me the text was not important, I was supposed to write it for all those who will come after. Will there be any after?

Once the demons are chased away, will I hear other stories again? If I do not write that book, I will no longer write, silence will have won, this silence that irritates Eli. Too often he believes that I do not want to speak when in fact I cannot.

Before, I used to think that I could write. Perhaps the chosen medium is inadequate, uncomfortable? But it is a part of the whole ruled by this fear. I have begun to write the text in the third person, to hide myself, and I am aware this camouflage is ridiculous, my fingers write: "she", "him" while my head is thinking "I", "Paul". Between the two, a mental block. But it is not enough to write "I" for the multiple gags to drop, these successive layers of masks with which I ridiculously dress up my characters. And I think of the curve with fondness! I feel, for the first time, the need to tell, to tell it all, absolutely all the stories that are in my head. I react as if I were still conditioned by my lifelong habit of silence! Not to speak about just anything to just anyone, you never know whom you are dealing with. Paranoia cultivated by the instinct of self-preservation, this lifelong attitude had disappeared I thought; it comes back under another guise. I no longer want to hide! I no longer need to hide, I no longer must be afraid but I must find a way to remove the masks. Always the masks. It is not a question of being careful, not to say too much, on the contrary, I need to say too much, to find the way to convey this command to my fingers, it is a question of survival, I can no longer bear to remain silent. I know I talk alone, sometimes in a loud voice, more often deep inside myself, but I need to write this text: never mind cautiousness, there will always be someone to prevent me from committing the unforgivable mistakes, if I really succeed in giving up my habits of self-censorship. I am going to start all over again, including the few pages written in the first person, a timid attempt to begin the exorcism. I am going to write and then I will have Paul read the text: if it is necessary to suppress, delete, erase, correct, I will do it then. I am going to tell Paul my stories as if he were here. I know it will be different: in his presence I will put on the mask again, I will become silent again. Besides if I was able to show him the first pages, it was thanks to the camouflage. He has removed it as if it was useless! I am going to write as if I were writing for a child to whom I will give birth, never mind if the false issues reappear, if the hang-ups come back when I expect them the least, never mind if everything is distorted right at the beginning, I have no choice. I will write for the same one, always the same one, always the same ones. I must write for those who are not short of reading material. Despite everything, I will write the story for Paul, and my stories for Maya, my still unborn daughter.

The Beheaded Statue

A little girl was named Paul, but everybody called her Lili. Why? It's a long story. When she was born, her parents wanted the baby to be a boy (they have always denied it, but she knows the truth), so they named her Paul. The mother, who claims responsibility for the choice of this name, says that it just happened due to the mistake of the semi-literate clerk who filled out the form, that the little girl should have been named Paule (the "e" might have changed many things). In any case, mistake or not, what does it matter since everybody called her Lili. Someone even made the bold assertion that she gave herself that nickname, that it explains her name change, as if adults concern themselves with what little girls may devise! In all likelihood, it suited them that the little girl changed her name. Much later, when the little girl, then an adult, decided to recover her real identity, they all opposed it. Some saying that habits are tenacious, others that her name was not important (then why was it changed?). It was important to her but that is another story. I only want to talk of the little girl.

When she was born, her father lived in a big, cold city in a big, misty and rainy country. Her mother, who had stayed back home, was expecting the baby. Mothers are always waiting! A few months after this birth, long months for her, ten too short months for a tiny baby, the mother left to rejoin the father. This is why, on top of a father and a mother, she was given substitutes. Jacques was her godfather, her substitute father, in sequential order. (As for her godmother, she has never known her, nor has she ever known her name. For her, she was the sister of the artist whose picture adorned the dining room. She did not feel any loss; godmothers are of no use especially when one has two mothers). The little girl, then, lived with Jacques and Marie.(Some episodes of this childhood have been related, but little girls never remember their childhood. Those I want to remember, Lili has recovered in the drawers of her memory, by herself.) A crying fit, violent, about her parents going out. Marie and Jacques had gotten her used to their constant presence, and since little girls quickly become selfish, she demanded this presence. There were also the outings she was included in, those evenings at the open air cinema when, on the way back, she fell asleep in the car and woke up in Jacques' arms. He carried her to the bedroom, their bedroom to the three of them, and she would agree to go back to sleep only after their promise to tell her, upon waking up, the story of the movie they had just seen together. And then, a stay at Le Cap, and here her memories blur with the stories told by Marie: the house with the balcony overhanging above the narrow street from where she used to throw her brand-new toys to the children passing by. More tears, the jeep taking away the adults while she felt excluded. She remained alone in front of a small house surrounded by flowers and fruit trees. But above all, the walks in a square.

She had gone out that day with someone who must have been her nanny. They had left for a walk in the square. It was the end of the afternoon, the square was located near the sea or a river. It was the sea! The little girl was happy to be strolling there; she looked at the water, the flowers and the trees. She was telling her nanny what the birds were telling her. Both of them were having great fun; birds tell such amusing stories, they see lots of things that happen in town and they are nosy, the birds are. When, in the square, at the time people go out for a stroll, they encounter a little girl then they start repeating what they have seen or heard. Since this little girl listened to them, they kept on talking. She liked their babbling and stayed hours on a bench in the square near the sea, very still, so as not to disturb the birds. Lili knew that birds dislike people who move around, people who stir the air forcing them to fly away. She would reach the center of the square, sit on a bench, like a stone statue, tell those around her not to move and keep quiet; then, the birds would come close: the first one perched on her lap, the second on her shoulder, the third who liked to nestle settled on her hair, and the others, in small groups, alighted around the bench. It was a ritual which was repeated every day they took a walk.

The first time, the nanny wanted to chat with a friend, so she had sat the little girl on a wooden bench, telling her to be good and to wait for her. Knowing that she could be good only if asleep, the little girl had leaned against the back of the bench and closed her eyes to keep her promise. She then sensed the arrival of the birds. But a promise is sacred, she did not move. When they were all there, she merely opened her eyes and smiled at them.

— Hello birds, I am sitting quietly and waiting.

— I see! What is your name?

— Paul, without an "e," but grown-ups call me Lili. It comes from Poli that they have changed into Lili, you understand?

— It is complicated. We will call you little girl. Each time you will come for a walk, if you do not frighten us, we will tell you some stories. If you want, we will start right now.

That day, they did not have the time. Lots of people arrived. They were entering the park, running all over the place. They were shouting loudly. The birds left. Lili was watching all these people and wondering what could make them run like that? The nanny came back, grabbed her by one hand and she too started to run, dragging along the little girl. She did not want to, the nanny had to take her into her arms to go fast. It is then that the little girl saw what all these loud people were doing: they were heading toward the statue by the sea. A very tall man took a very long rope, wrapped it around the neck of the statue, a woman behind tied a knot and the others started to pull until the statue, beheaded, falls into the sea. And they were shouting with joy when the head fell in with lots of water bursting forth, people assembled in big circles. The nanny left the square, still running and carrying the little girl in her arms; she stopped only at the sight of the house with the balcony. Afterward, their walks were peaceful and the little girl was able to continue talking quietly to the birds. This story may have taken place in 1957, but the little girl did not know the date.

It was in 1957, she was then six years old, she was therefore a very little girl unaware of what was going on, living in her own world. Her life went on peacefully, without any changes. However, two events briefly disturbed Lili's peaceful life. First the return of this man she did not know, it was Paul but she didn't know him. She had not heard about his leaving, but one day he came back. The grown-ups were whispering, keeping silent when the little girl came in (as if she were interested in their secrets!). Once more, Paul was asked to be nice, good, and the man took her in his arms. He held her very tightly, kissing her, but she wanted so much to be put down. Nevertheless she remained good. He kissed her and his kisses pricked her. Paul's beard was all over his face: the beard of a father pricks a lot when the beard is short and when the father kisses strongly. It tickles too! The little girl did not dare to scratch her neck; she had been asked to be good.

The other event that disrupted Paul's habits was that story with Jacques. She understood nothing; for her, the adults were playing. She did not know why she was not allowed to enter the bedroom. Yet, she liked the new bedrooms at the homes of the new grown-ups. Jacques was lying on a small bed, too small for him, a kerchief around his head. She thought he was funny. Since little girls are curious,

Paul had immediately noticed the hole in the partition. Or was it the keyhole? No, she was not patient enough to discover the keyhole; it was just a hole in the partition. So she watched everything. There were other children with her and they too found Jacques amusing. But afterward, Marie cried and the little girl didn't understand. Seeing the woman crying all the time, Lili was becoming sad, crying also, without knowing why. Fortunately, Marie's friends were saying: "Look, you are making Lili cry (her friends also called her Lili), stop, you are influencing this child. Be brave, at least for her sake." One day, Marie stopped crying so she would not cause incomprehensible pain to the little girl. Maybe she was still doing it, but she was hiding it well; at times, when Lili observed her closely, she could see that the white of her eyes was red.

The beard and the eyes have remained in the drawers. The other she has not filed, and yet it is the only one that she still keeps, odious scar that nothing can erase. He had come, with other men, because of a long story that the little girl did not know. He had made a long journey. They had not even fired a shot, they were not many, not strong, not ready, above all alone, and when they were fired at, they stayed alone and died alone. They had not understood that they would be alone; it was their mistake because they had understood nothing. It is difficult to destroy such an illusion; like him, others imagine they can do it all alone, for the others (they said, they say, they will go on saying for a long time), instead of the others, without wanting to understand that the others also know. Contempt? No, too long a practice. Since then the little girl no longer talks to the birds, their stories do not amuse her.

∽∾∾

A different town. Another house. All houses do not look alike. And yet, they end up blending. The balcony overlooking a narrow street. From this temporary home will remain only the balcony and this child standing up. She looks down to the street and watches the others. First glances. She was throwing her presents from the balcony. She will be told that they were toys. Does it matter? The first gesture of discomfort. The first expression of this difference whose screaming in her head will never stop. Sole memory of the northern city where it all began. With another more blurred and persistent. This square by the seaside, this quay, this pier, and a popular demonstration, the rumblings of a crowd throwing a statue tied up to an enormous rope into the ocean. Has the woman dragged away the little girl to shelter her? Of this woman, nothing. A silhouette in black and blue. A silhouette of which nothing remains?

Death. Death? She was laughing. Through the hole in the partition she was looking at this man. Later, she will dream of him. He will be handsome with a round face and blue eyes. Why blue? She will never understand. Blue like the bedroom of the woman crying. Death is a word. Death meant nothing. She had not yet met death in everyday life. Maybe in books; if so it had no significance. Furthermore, the little girl could not read. Later, they will explain to her the death of a man whose body will never be found; the face on the photograph that she saw from her chair at the table. An unknown dead man? Or the dead man seen through the partition of the bedroom? She knew this man without knowing him, she lived with him. At an age when one is not aware of death, does one already know the living? She would have met him later, in her memories, but at the time of her recollection, he was no longer there. She came to know this man through the memory of a woman. Death. His face strangely calm, his head wrapped in a white cloth filled the entire width of the hole; she sees nothing else and she laughs. Tears will come later. Tears will be shed. Not for this dead man, neither for the pain. Tears for the woman, because of the woman. She was discovering an unhappy woman and she was crying. Oblivion came. Oblivion dries tears, and in front of her eyes faces will flash by. She will know later that it was the beginning of the great madness. Strangers arriving at night. Strangers hiding in a dark room of the house. The yellow bathroom. Why does she think of it as dark? In full daylight, this room gets the sun. A peculiar bathroom with a small bed and a large desk. Strangers would hide during the day. The room stayed dark or closed. These strangers who jumped at the slightest noise, who spoke in a whisper. Among those who had succeeded in fleeing. Among those who, like them, were hiding away. Among those we knew nothing about. Among those who, we knew too well, would never come back. As for her, she shouted, stamped her feet in the big house. The strangers and their single room upstairs. She would run from top to bottom in the big house. Then, one day, she became part of the strangers. Then one night, she followed the woman in a dark room. She did not understand. She was accompanying the woman. Going out at night, with furtive gestures, living shut-in during the day, and she laughed. She played at being on vacation. She was still playing when the man with the bearded cheeks arrived. The beard that pricked. She will know, long after, the reasons of this thin and bearded man. Later, she will know the number of days he spent in a dark room, but he did not go out at night. Later, she will know, but these were carefree days, nothing could affect her laughter, her days of non-memory. It will come with a slap that hurt her in her body and in her heart; a lesson of survival for her, who had just come out of the path of innocence. A slap for her, who was discovering the softness of her body on a man's lap, a slap teaching her that there were words she should not utter, glances to be veiled. And then, everything came back to her at once: the awareness of the death of those she had not had the time to know, the beard of this man absent for forty days. Forty days, she repeated for a long time, without noticing anything. And all of a sudden, the memory comes back: "He stayed forty days and forty nights...." The absent man was not the messiah, but forty days won him complete forgiveness. Except for her revolt when this man talked to her of heritage. This man saying that she was his son. The revolt forgotten when the time comes to understand. This slap gives life to the legitimate daughter. And when the experience of horror comes back, the child will have had the time to harden herself.

Now, I feel well. I may decide once again to alter the pages already written but it will be with serenity. I remember a story called "Berceuse," a tale I enjoyed writing, I even liked to read over; does the form of the tale allow me to tell my stories? Storytelling is perhaps the form very close to what I feel when I tell them in my head. Then I will write tales for Maya.

I feel more at ease tonight. I feel a coordination between my fingers and my head, and, at the same time, a loosening, an absence of tension, a strange sensation of freedom. The act of writing about Jacques, about feeling less powerless when thinking of him, about this first con-tact with a dead man who must have been the cause of my attitude to always face death, who certainly influ-enced my standpoint. I always think of Claudine's reac-tions who, at the age of 30, for the first time has been affected by it. I understand her, but at Eva's death, I saw it differently. The laughter of a little girl, the nearness of Marie's pain at a time when I could not really know this pain, have conditioned me. The reactions I understand, but I refuse to share them. To bewail, to cry, to make myself miserable at the death of somebody one knows, appreciates, respects, or loves I do not want. I would know not to cry for the one who is dead, but at finding myself alone. They (who often represent the average per-son) say that death is unfair. In the name of what justice? Do they think (but "they" do not think) only about what the person might have accomplished? I doubt it. Most people who cry think only about their petty selfish interests. I hate this hypocrisy which makes them say "she died so young when I have already lived, I should have died in her place." Obviously, if one is a criminal, an exploiter, a child or an adult torturer, but in this case, no! one would not want to die. When Eva died, of course I was sad, because I thought of her presence that I would no longer have, of her example of a strong woman, of the solitude of Marie who found herself without her partner, but I also thought "she lived as she wished, she accomplished what she deemed useful, I hope, to the extent of her limits and her abilities, others will take over, others will go further, I will go further." It will always be that way, it must always be that way. (If I cried at Ernesto's death, it was the sadness of a sentimental little girl, but, not knowing him, being linked to this man neither by blood nor by land nor by choice, already I shed the only tears I will be capable of. (Gratuitous!)

I no longer remember even my grandmother's death. Still, I keep the memory of that woman, the gentleness of a wrinkled face. I see her lying on a little bed, in a corner of the pink room, small, shrunken, looking up at my few centimeters with tenderness. A little girl freshly powdered, in a little white linen dress, with white taffeta ribbons in her hair, I would go and kiss that old woman before going out for a stroll. She would remain

43

lying there, always lying down, sick, close to death, and I will not even remember the day when she was no longer there. But one image will be hateful to me. When unhappy in a waiting room, I will recall this voice telling me "be careful, see a doctor for these migraines, for these fainting spells, these noises in your head, your grandmother died of head pains, [voice lowered] I even think that she had become...." The voice did not go on hoping that through this allusion the poison would work... I would laugh out loud and accepted it with joy. Crazy grandmother, mad, they said! Well, even better! I claim this mad woman who raised all these children: thirteen! Carried, gave birth to, cared for, cradled, educated, scolded, loved; one is entitled to madness, to this mad woman lying on a little iron bed, looking up with tenderness at a little girl dressed in white linen. This madness transmitted to Paul along with the rage to live, this madness passed in his blood along with love, the inheritance of the no, of the refusal to accept that once and for all everything was over. I know that she did not have the choice, no other choice but these thirteen children, with a house, a husband, meals to prepare, clothes to mend, servants (to oppress a little more when one has suffered oppression?). I know that I refuse that life, but I refuse anyone the right to think they can frighten me, shame me, horrify me with the specter of the probable madness of a dead person.

But I no longer want to think about it, I no longer want to be swept by anger.

The Incredible Yet True Story of a Little Girl Who Had Many Mothers But Only One Father To Make Her Cry...

This is the story of a very little girl. She does not yet know how to be a child and a girl, no one has made her feel like one, she has just been born and knows nothing. Like all babies who have just been born, she has a mother (almost all babies do). Sometimes, the mother dies immediately but this was not the case with the little girl. Therefore she had a mother, and an absent father. Fathers are often absent either because they do not want the baby (this is common) or because they have to be away for they are men and men have more important things than a baby (this is very common) or they die, but this is less common than for mothers. Sometimes, fathers are present but this was not the case. Thus after the birth of the little girl, her mother looks at her. She must have looked happy, mothers normally do, but deep down she finds the baby very ugly. She says nothing because that is not done. She asks someone to go and register the baby, all babies must be registered or they do not exist. Strange, but grown-ups have funny ideas. Even though the mother found the little girl ugly, she wanted her to be registered. So someone went and registered her under the name of Paul, a strange name for a little girl but this is another story. When they left the hospital, the mother and the little girl lived together for a few months, then the mother left to be with the absent father. She could have brought Paul with her but it was too complicated. Since she was a tiny baby, she had to be entrusted to someone; a baby cannot survive alone, a mother is needed. Marie, being childless, agreed to take care of the little girl and became her interim mother. The little girl then had two mothers. In theory only, because in reality, she only had one mother. She grew up and only knew Marie. The other one was very far away at first, and then upon her return she did not take back the little girl who was still as ugly. However, she agreed to meet her often (Julia says it was not necessary to take her away from Marie; this was a beautiful gesture on her part, Marie will love her even more), the little girl grew up with her everyday mother and her Sunday mother. There was Jacques, but he did not stay long enough in the story, she did not know him well enough to make him her everyday father. Would everything have occurred differently, then, if she had had as many fathers to balance out the women in her life?

One day, finally the little girl had a little sister. There was already the child of the Sunday mother but that was normal: each mother had an everyday little girl who became the Sunday little girl of the other mother. Suddenly, another little sister. And another woman! The little girl did not understand who that woman could be. Of course, she came to realize that it was another, who also had two daughters. The whole thing did not go smoothly. The only father decided that the interim period had lasted long enough, and that he and the new mother (therefore the third) decided to take the little girl back. For a long time she kept a grudge against them for having made Marie cry, she could not stand those tears, she felt responsible for those tears and could not do anything. Marie was crying to see her everyday little girl go. She found this separation unfair. Paul thought that it was sad, because of Marie, because if she had been by herself, she would have been brave, little girls are brave when they know they are the weakest. But adults are so fragile! When they are distressed, they must be protected, consoled, and the little girl tried her best to console Marie. Sometimes, in spite of everything, she felt powerless. There was, in addition to Marie's tears, the non-tears of the father even more difficult to console. This was at the very beginning.

She had understood that her life at school had taken a new direction. When in the morning, she arrived, her hair not neatly done, her cousin Mireille wanted to do her braids over and she said nothing. She cared little that Jeanne did not do her hair before she left for school; she was learning how to get by alone. It was tough sometimes but she got used to it gradually, she managed to dress herself, put on her socks, lace her boots, black boots white socks, the only pair, that she washed everyday. When Paul found out, she was entitled to the speech "I can buy you new shoes, you only have to ask, etc... etc... ." She had not thought about it. In those days, without being taught, without understanding the problems large and small of her parents, Lili had felt she had to be reasonable. No one had explained to her that her father had lost his job on account of that story of the forty days of absence; no one had commented that he was having a hard time making a living, no one had shown her that the little house at *Tête de l'Eau* was a house of difficult times, no one had told the little girl that she had to be reasonable, especially not Paul, and yet she was not asking for a single new dress, for a single extravagant toy, not even for an extra pair of socks, she simply had not thought about it. She no longer ever thinks about that period, that awful house, she keeps only a few images at the back of her head: concrete everywhere, the dining-room with the stairs leading up, the room where the four little girls slept, the door communicating with the other room, small also, where her parents slept. The entrance, also cement (sometimes I see it in horrible nightmares), gently sloping down to the three steps where she sat to play with her doll. It did not matter to have only one pair of socks, or to be forced to cross the ravine with Carole, at nightfall, both dying of fright, to go and get the bread. From that period, the little girl will keep the tender or funny images. Deliberately? The first time when Annie crossed the room on her little legs, awkward and smiling in her shoes with little bells (everyone could hear her steps), the night when Carole swallowed some detergent, thinking she was putting vinegar on her salad, and Rachel's tears at the sight of the panic-stricken faces. They had been forbidden to use vinegar and they loved their salads highly seasoned. (Paul will keep the taste of salads too highly seasoned.) Carole had to swallow a huge glass of milk to avoid being poisoned. (She still hates milk!). Paul will say later "it was a difficult period." For the little girl it was something else: going to St. Peter's church alone, because no one else went, not daring to enter, she would attend mass standing up, leaning sideways against a door. On Sundays, she always wore a white organdy dress that resisted wear and tear and that gave her the look of a Carnival queen. Bad hairstyle and bad shoes, she could not care less. That was the year of Marie's tears, of the impossible choice to make, she could not decide who was wrong and who was right.

To choose on the day of the party was cruel: he had brought her over to wish Marie a happy birthday, and at the outset of the evening, he had come to pick her up. The woman was crying to see her go. The child had entered the car silently. And Mireille said: Please, Uncle Paul, let her sleep over at Marie's. Mireille dared to speak. And he put his head on the wheel. Get out, if you want. She said no, she could not choose and he was giving her the choice. Then Mireille took her by the hand and Lili followed her older cousin. She did not turn back hoping he would leave before she reached the front door, but he was not leaving, she could not hear the noise of the car. At the door, she looked back. He still had his forehead against the wheel. She began to cry. Later she will be proud to have several mothers. That day, she felt mostly torn. Because of her, there were the tears of Marie and the non-tears of Paul. Later, she will laugh to tears when people will say "you are your mother's daughter. You resemble her a lot" which one? but people were right. Yet they could not understand the spark in her eyes and her teasing smile. Later, she will always say my sister speaking of Rachel and of Carole, my twin, do you know her? And they are her sisters. That day, she did not dare, they were the daughters of the other one. Later, she will have fun explaining her strange family: you know, my mother who is my almost godmother, my little sister who is my half-sister, my father's daughter and ...(or my mother's daughter and...) my mother who is not my mother is my father's wife and therefore my mother, of course I am referring to Jeanne. You know, Julia is my mother. Which one? Come on now! My real mother, the one who is more my friend than maternally mine. People would get confused, and she would laugh out even more, the transition was much too painful, the strange family will come later, much later after this period soaked with Marie's tears. And the little girl will keep her taste for complicated families.

(Carole, my darling, you must meet my brother. Your brother, she says laughing, we do not have a brother except of course this mythical brother who lives elsewhere that Paul has told us about. Yes, my sister, we do not have a brother, while having a brother, but I have adopted one. Why not? I no longer wanted him for a lover, and I loved him too much not to keep him in my life. I want to introduce you to Steve. After all, it was not fair, a brother was missing in our strange family.)

৵৶

Uprooted. Playing the martyr with sincerity. She believed it. She detested the whole thing. Because of Marie. The little concrete house. The trips on foot. The nighttime crossings of the ravine. Later, the other house, large and cool. The walls. The mosaics. The doors too heavy for her skinny little girl wrists. The stares of these boys perched on the wall. The man. The woman. The weather. She was born in 1951. In 1957, she would have been six years old. In those days, it became unbearable. The day of her birthday, or perhaps a few days before or after, she turned one hundred years old, or maybe older. Who would have suspected it?

She was growing up like all the other children in the world, but here, those who were already born could not be the same. They understood it, said nothing to the adults, avoided causing them even more problems. They had nothing against them. Yet, everything happened due to whose fault? She believed that, she was so gullible! With the wrinkles, she will end up recognizing her error. She will make the mistake? It does not matter. One must not bear her a grudge. The example had been too beautiful, they spent their lives getting drunk on words; they took for granted the right to be proud, and did not care about protecting the heritage. The child will understand only much later, far away, when her hatred will turn to contempt, when her anger will come with love, that the names of the guilty mattered little. But in those days, there was an urgency to learn (in that house too big), to no longer fear the dark, to learn to laugh when, outside, the noise of the firearms sounds like the one coming from the exhaust pipes of the rare cars, to laugh at the frightful knowledge that friends, an uncle, a mother, have left the world of the walking dead. With time, she will know she had never been a show-off. The horror had become natural! The adults will reproach her for her indifference, her cruelty, they will never understand that she had nothing to lose but her weakness.

Where to begin? Symbols, these different colored homes, symbols found later on in order to explain. Why explain it all? Multiple questions. She replies: it was a woman. My mother? A woman was the first to act. A woman looks at the other woman lying down, a smile on her lips, closeness, knowing glances of those who know, and the last contraction, and the skillful hands of a woman pulling out the warm and humid body from her first house. The triumphant laugh! A woman holds in her hands a body that will become a woman. May her spirit be spared! The one lying down knows the scars of this future too close. She believes in a different future. That one, out of her womb, will not become a woman regretting to be born. Did she already know, the one lying down that the repetition was over? Did she already know that this child would not become a woman? She was born a child and would remain so. Never to be polished into becoming one. The rejection of the whole thing.

Often hidden in a word, a scent or a gesture, I find the green house again, I return to the green house. The first days, the daily life, the anxieties, my departure come back to me from the depths of forgotten drawers. A gesture of Eli running us a bath makes me relive this panic of the first day. A general bath. Jeanne had decided to give us a bath outside. I refused to take my clothes off. It had come with the first learned gestures, the modesty passed down, which was part of my habits, a modesty that had become natural. And the shock! When he takes my clothes off, I see this little girl again, refusing to take off these clothes that shield her. Against what? The look of the others, the taboos of the others? This child reacting the way she is supposed to. And Jeanne's determination (am I forcing this memory?), was it the right approach? The outcome was positive, but at the moment of contact with the water, this rage inside my head, a pain hovering on top of the memories of my first days in the house, this shame in the presence of these two boys perched on the dividing wall. We will laugh about it later, taboos gone, modesty unlearned. And yet, and yet I am still looking at my hand searching for the switch for all these rooms: I turn the light off, as if to say no again to Jeanne. Faced with their protests, I feel the taste of ancient tears and this desire to die. More than death, in the back of my head, in close-up, my hatred for the other one. Am I making this up? No, there was that hatred that had also been passed on, hatred for this unfamiliar woman who had torn me away from the familiar tenderness. And I will laugh! It was out of the question to laugh about this little tub with its minuscule faucet and the cool water which burns my naked skin, the sun which freezes the inside of my stomach and the relief which comes with a towel drying the water and my tears. And my anger! I will learn to love this woman, this usurper so much that even today a feeling of betrayal still stays with me. Mother, three faces of women, three ways of loving, three faces of a little girl that swirl around in all directions. I sail through these mirrors no longer knowing which image is real. And might all three of them be but masks put on by the glances of these three women on a skinny and ugly girl? And might this search for the early days in the green house be a quest for the real face hidden underneath the three masks? Janus with the two faces, he said that I was Janus with the two faces, playing on my masculine name and the weakness he guessed in me. As for me, I wish for Janus with three faces because there are three women.

I am lying, lying. The importance of these women is in inverse proportion to their number, they could have been a hundred that I would have had two faces; one for him, one for me. The three women's images float in my head, in the stories I tell myself, and it is always mostly about him! I detest Freud! Why do girls give such an enormous place to Man? These superb women that I love, these women who struggle, found the answer before I was born to feminine consciousness. The power? The power! In spite of everything, I feel something else deep inside myself; for me it's not about a man but about him, Paul, I will end up writing about him. I change course, I cover up my tracks, I conceal the name, I invent stories so as not to find him again, I call him "he," the "silent man" and the stories I write all tell a long story in which he is the one, the one who... the one who has taught me to be strong, the one who has shown me hatred through a look and a hand gesture. The one who, like Eli, understands my hatred for the man in black, the man whose name must not be mentioned, the man who is everywhere and one must not see, the man Maya will never know but will have to be told about, not because he was the man who dressed in black, but for who he is: the man in black, the man symbol, the man logical continuation of a long line of other men in black even if they wore all the colors of the prism.

The Man in Black

Once upon a time, in another time, a little girl had grown up. She had been going to school for some time now and liked it. This little girl was curious, all curious little girls love school. She listened to the grown-ups, especially when they talked in a low voice, hearing things that she should have never learned. Why be sad when one is ten years old, goes to school, does her homework diligently, when the sun shines and one does not have a care in the world? But it was too late, she already knew too much. She hid it well, though, not only from those who were not supposed to guess anything but from her parents, her friends, to all of those who looked at her placid face. She was for them the little girl who went to school, who came home for lunch at noontime and did her homework in the afternoon. To better hide what she knew, she studied a great deal, got good grades in school, thus no one suspected her. She was very careful: one time, however, she made a mistake. She thought she could trust her best friend and she should not have. (She will quickly unlearn trust!) She had told her friend what she had overheard, that her uncle was not a good man, because.... The friend repeated everything to her uncle. Adults get upset when one tells a little truth, the uncle got upset. The father of the little girl ordered her to apologize. Later, she will understand that no one is ever completely good or completely bad; but at that moment, she did not, the little girl was very sad and felt betrayed. She knew that her father did not think she had lied, she had only repeated words overheard: "He is a bogeyman!" Since her father blamed her, the little girl understood that it was much more preferable to hide her feelings. She continued to get good grades in school. She concealed her true self so well that even the man in black was not able to read the real reason for her unblinking stare. The man in black was someone whom everybody knew but who was not to be named; if one spoke of him, one had to be very careful, always speak well of him, and for those who chose to say those lies not to make a mistake, no one should find out about the lie. As for the little girl, she was taught not to say anything.

She had already seen the face of the man in black, everybody saw him at one time or another. He was everywhere. When the little girl will read *1984*, the character of Big Brother will remind her of the man in black. But Big Brother, no one will ever see him. The man in black, she saw him one day, from up close. She was on her way to school: and to get there, each day, she took the same path. They were no other paths as direct. Besides, she loved that way because she could look at the trees, and dip her fingertips in the water fountain. One morning, she left home earlier than usual, carrying at arm's length her schoolbag full of books and notebooks, walking very slowly. She had often wondered if the man was already up at that time. It was seven o'clock. In front of the man's house with the white walls, she slowed down; at the gate, she stopped, a car was coming out, and it was prudent to wait. She kept looking down, it was better not to see anything. While she waited by the side of the front gate for the moment to cross over, she daydreamed. If she only possessed magical powers, like the women of the evenings of storytelling, she would look up and know who sat in that car. She would see the man in black trembling with fear upon recognizing her. She would use her magic to turn him into a grass snake, he deserved nothing else! The little girl smiled inside, thinking that would be a good action. She waited and the car did not go by. She then looked up, and it is him. The man in black is seated inside the car, a few steps away from her, looking at her. The little girl is afraid. She sees him and her hatred swirls around her. He smiles at her and she wants to die. To die because she cannot destroy that smile. He waves to her to cross over and she smiles in turn, while thinking in her head "I hate him," "I hate him!," like an incantation, like the utterance of a little girl who knows too much, naive but armed with a premonitory sensibility. The man could not guess what she was thinking, he must have said to himself, "Look, a little girl," and that's all. She went on her way, a hand in her pocket, so no one would notice, the trembling of her entire body, and the other hand tightly gripping the handle of her bag that suddenly weighed twice as much.

ॐ

Morning sunshine. She is walking. She thinks, "I am not late." In those days, time still mattered. She crosses the square. On that morning under the sun, she does not cross the street. She goes along the sidewalk in front of the house with the whitewashed walls. The gate opens, a large car moves into the narrow path. The child stops. The car slows down. The passenger waves for her to cross over. She bends her head and continues. Did she smile? Probably. The woman who is older wanted that smile. To add on to the remorse? The little girl was not thinking about the picture on the brick wall. The dead traveler. The hero's picture at eye level at mealtime. All the rooms have a special color: the small green sitting room, the red kitchen, the pink bathroom, the other, yellow, brings back to mind the dark memories, the blue bedroom. All the bedrooms will be blue because for the little child a bedroom can only be blue. It will take time to forget. But a black outfit. But the pain in her head? What can time do? The child will never want to, she does not have the right. It is not about knowing whether the memory stays, memory has nothing to do with it.

Every day, the child takes the same path. A hot path bearable only in the morning? Does it rain often? Under the looks of the passers-by, the bronze statues keep their impassive expressions. The trees, the shade she looks for on the hottest days. Rarely. She prefers the sidewalk. The asphalt burns her bare feet. She has taken her shoes off to shock the others. Was it at the time of the smile of the man in black? No, the bare feet will come later. The child goes on her way. He goes by. She looks at him. Why will she never forget that day? The child will grow up, the man will go by, but the child will never forget. That smile will not erase the memory of a slap for another look, a slap which will burn her inside and out, a slap to save her life. The look of the child, the look defying fear. The father understood that he had to erase it, to remove death from this look, from her eyes. He will explain the slap. Did she understand? She knew nothing about the others, she did not understand the possibility of an easy lesson. She did not believe in the proximity of death.

To hide, she very quickly learned that it was imperative for her to hide her self, she very quickly understood that just like words, gestures and even looks betrayed. It was in the mountains. Another house, the house of the uncle gone far away. The little girl did not like that house where the furniture, and the dressers full of clothes, the smoothly stretched bedspreads, everything pointed to a hasty departure. And it was there that, one evening, the pain struck. She has never understood what happened. She was listening to them speaking, a conversation between grown-ups, with harsh words. The little girl knew that it was about those things one does not repeat, even to one's best friend. André spoke. There was a long silence. She moved, looked at the man. A few seconds after, the slap. Paul had struck her, she did not understand. She ran away to the bedroom. Noise of voices. The door opening and Paul's voice. She was crying. He stroked her hair. I beg your pardon. Try to understand, if you can. André spoke. You looked at him with such contempt. I saw you dead. I know now that you could not grasp the meaning of the words pronounced. You did not do it on purpose. You do not like André. I saw in a flash that you looked at a bogeyman that way. He was killing you. You had to be protected. Forgive me when you can. She did not know the meaning of the words. She did not like André, she will never forgive him for the slap. It was the first time. There will not be a second slap. She forgave and understood that she had to hide her true self even better.

I have not written anything for several days. I had started writing a few lines one evening, coming back from work, but Eli called and I left to go and see him. I stayed in the apartment the entire weekend, getting used to them, developing a liking for this different way of life, for this constant activity around me. The days with them: people coming and going at any time, the door always open, there is no key at the front door of the apartment, in the street of L'Ours Blanc. There is no possible outer solitude and this does not bother me. My inner solitude, which comes back too often in spite of my numerous evasions, resists the presence of all these people, the noise, even the bustle of this noisy street. I am getting used to it and I feel a tenderness for them, this cheerful and joyous tribe. There is however a hint of sadness hidden deep down in every member's eyes. I recognize their untold fears and their anger. I know this shield. They burst out laughing, everything is blotted out. The clan is strong, the tribe is an effective protection but a dangerous one. I sense that the story pushed to its limits, with them all, would be impossible. I often feel like writing their stories, their laughter, and this silence one feels in the middle of the party. I feel like describing them in the sun and the swirling snow. I would love to get to know them all, to have time to spend with them, to love each in turn but I cannot: either I write about them or I live with them. I am afraid to scatter myself and I am ashamed of so much pettiness. It is already difficult with Eli, I ask too much of his attention in order to compensate for this feeling of betrayal toward the text, I demand his presence for a page that stays blank. I have not written anything during the long winter evenings at the apartment of L'Ours Blanc.

And tonight, coming back from the demonstration, I had the desire to shut myself away, to isolate myself, to create a vacuum in order to regain my memories. I am tense and I do not want to explode. I know that they will not understand, they are still feeling the euphoria of that huge crowd, expected, yet unexpected, surprising. I am not reticent, I do not reject the gestures, I only have a bitter taste in my mouth, the nagging doubt. What do we know of political prisoners in Chile, snug in our winter coats? Of course, I hear their speeches describing the impact of the exiles' organizations. Can one stop the suffering of political prisoners? Can one stop the existence of political prisoners? Can one? I listen to their answers full of assurances, but what do we know...?

The Little Dog Is Dead

It is night time. The green house is completely silent and outside the dogs are barking. In the room, a little girl sleeps. She spent a long time with her schoolbooks and this occupation tired her. She sleeps and outside the dogs are barking. Without making a noise, the father steps out of the library. First he turned off the record player, put away his newspaper, he is going to bed. Before he does, as all the other evenings, he will go and unwind watching his girls sleeping. Four girls in a house, four girls in the little bedroom. She, the one named Paul but that everyone calls Lili, forces the father to continue with his ritual. Before he reaches his bedroom, he goes by the little room to listen to their regular breathing, to smile at their four peaceful and secretive faces and to cover up again the body of a little girl. She tosses and turns a lot in her sleep and constantly throws back the bed sheets that he insists on pulling up over her skinny shoulders. She turns around and he sees her face. Her face is sad. The father asks himself what the sad-faced little girl, who tosses around so much in her sleep, could be dreaming of. He runs his fingers on her open lips. She opens her eyes and he sees fear. She opens her eyes without seeing him and says "Pépé." The father realizes then that she is dreaming about the little dog poisoned to death the day before. By whom, the father ignores and so does the little girl. She still denies the disappearance of Pépé. In her dream, she sees the dog in the arms of her youngest sister. She smiles, settles back to her reading, not wishing to join them.

"Tibobo Pépé," the little girl speaks to the dog and Paul smiles. She no longer sees them but overhears the voice of the little sister. She hears, a while later, the cries of the dog and goes out. Tibobo Pépé, she understands the words, the sequence of words which are meaningless. Tibobo Pépé, the language of a world still accessible to the universe of six-year old Annie, and Pépé the dog, being trained behind the gates of the old green house, it is easy to understand! The gestures, the stick raised towards the dog, a stick which attacks the animal between the bars of the wrought iron gate, a stick held by ten griping fingers, what did the gestures mean? Was Annie already mimicking the world of those who did not want to see anything in Tibobo Pépé? Already the violence in what still resembles the unconscious: six years old, unconscious? What unconscious? The little girl knows how to be mean, she has already learned, she wants the dog to cry in pain, the powerless rage, the pawing of the air to stop the stick charging at him. Pépé barks barring his teeth, Pépé struck yelps in pain. The little girl laughing continues to play

Tibobo Pépé. She is dreaming that she is holding back her little sister. Still somewhere deep down in her mind, she knows she has played at hurting, but her memory does not want to recall, to relive the cruel gestures. She no longer knows, no longer wants to know, she even ignores whether she has ever accepted Pépé. Suddenly, the dog is no longer behind the gates. Paul realizes that he was not locked in, that he could have run away. He gets closer to Annie, who is crying, licking the tears on her face and the two of them leave to invent another game that occupies them the rest of the afternoon.

Paul smiles in her dream and, then, the scream. The father gets up again, runs toward the girls' bedroom. What is going on? Have you had a nightmare? It is my fault if Pépé is dead. No, says the father, we could not have guessed. Maybe, Pépé would not have died if I had accepted the leash. The father did not want to tie Pépé up. The little girls too preferred to see him run in the yard, barking to let them know when it was playtime. Did he want to play at Tibobo Pépé? Did he prefer the cruelty of the little sister to her indifference? She thinks about her father's words. If Pépé had had a leash? Never will she accept it. He has promised her another dog, she hopes he will forget this promise. She no longer wants a dog, no more Tibobo Pépé, no more leash for a little dead dog, she

73

does not want Pépé to disappear one day (and the cook says in a low voice "someone poisoned Pépé"). Someone has killed Pépé, someone has played too long at Tibobo Pépé. Pépé clean, well-fed, bright eyed, who refused to mix with the wandering starving dogs. Pépé who never flinched at the gesture of a hand picking up a rock, unschooled in the conditioned reflexes of the skinny dogs.

Sleep is long in coming. At what time began the terrible insomnia? How far back do they go -the first stories told night after night, cruel tales invented to find sleep, in order not to understand. Tossing in the little narrow bed, even in the middle of the month of July, refusing to put away the bedspread against the secret fears. And then, the tender stories in a low voice, the unknown body escaping the rules of gravity, dreaming, eyelids tightly shut, lips slightly open, about all these faces who in the morning are no longer alike. And she pressed her lips to her palm, kissing these faces whose contours are blurred. Sometimes the image of a little dead dog. Blurred image torn at the corners. She hears the dog barking.

Albinoni's *Adagio*. She fell asleep to the last measures of side A. She will have the impression of having heard it every evening of her life in the green house. He liked to listen to this record. Often. In the drawers of the little girl, the smell of tobacco and the record. He spent all his evenings in the library, by himself. She can recall only few friends. Alone, Jeanne too. No one came. They rarely went out. There was work to do, the children and the life away from prying eyes. Why can't she ever recall the faces, the names, the stable, solid, enduring presence of people. Around them, it was difficult to be trusting. The closeness, the cohesiveness of the little tribe, the protective clan that alone will provide a certain training. They even had the time to fight against certain nightmares. Certain ones, not all of them!

I had thought that this happiness had numbed my fingers. Gone the sweet pain, forever. These months of silence seemed to me filled with meaning, the source had dried up, I no longer needed the blank page. (Lined paper, graph paper, sheet already printed the back of which I used, I do not remember having used a blank page but the cliché remains.)

And the reunions! Anything that writes, on anything on which to write, I begin to be obsessed by the pen, I must have it always within my reach. That happiness has changed nothing, I keep my love for words. Still, life with the other one is taking over, I am aware of it. The other one, despite respect, despite independence and autonomy, has defined new frontiers. The other one and our common preoccupation: sharing this action, this wait for our destiny, sharing our new anger provoked by those who refuse to do anything, sharing our optimism with our new friends, the will to hold one of the pens that will write the story, not for us selfish and vain, but to safeguard love, to keep us from going mad. I begin to write again in spite of the distance, in spite of the hours of discouragement. Why slave away at turning these pages blue? Why these words lined up one after the other? Waste of time and energy! Why? For whom? Not for those we are thinking of; not for those toward whom we direct our steps on the other side of the frontiers of the dream. They do not know how to read this language I am using, because I do use it, with difficulty, although I feel it mine neither in my heart nor by right. But I cannot write in my native language as I would like to, not yet. If it was not so sad we could have all laughed about it. I did not learn, they did not let me ("they" this time pointing to those who thought they could imprison me in words alien to my native land in order to close my eyes), I will break those bars, never mind my clumsiness, my errors of syntax or spelling. Those I think about do not understand this language, they neither speak it nor write it. Why write? Because... they do not understand our common language other than coming out of our sealed mouths. I would have liked to write in my native tongue but they could not have been able to read me in Creole either. One day, I will know how to write and will begin again; one day, they will know how to read and will begin again. Until such time, I write to know, for this other one who is refusing the language as a tool whose words and structure I make mine. Domination, he says. I know. Exploitation, goes on Eli. I know, but "I also know." It's not the only one, what do you want me to do? To keep silent? I reject the silence, I continue, anyhow. Until the day comes when I know how to write, I practice writing, I learn. Until such time, I store the sentences I discover, an archivist, a usurer, I keep the story, little does it matter how, for the days of great sunshine.

The Insoluble Problem

Once upon a time, again, there was Paul still small since still going to school, still studious, doing her homework without making a fuss, meticulously. That afternoon, she was working on a math problem which had been keeping her busy for more than an hour; trains crossing (she has never seen a train), faucets refusing to fill immense tubs (she was thinking about the bucket, outside, getting warm in the sun; but reasonable, the little girl was doing her best to forget the water slowly running down her body in the middle of the yard, like the rain.)

The rain! She loved to stay in bed, listening to the raindrops on the metal roof, a funny noise, almost like music, since rain falls here in heavy drops beating on the sheets of light metal. Paul liked this sound and the coolness of the after-rain, the smell of wet earth from the tiny garden, its flowers bursting with fragrance in the returning sunshine. No one went out when it rained. Sometimes, the rain started when they were all gathered around the table and food tasted of holidays.

She is there near the window, listening to the rain and no longer seated at that table in front of the

painful homework, when suddenly sounds of voices
bring her back to it, distracting her, getting her attention. Lili goes down! The promise of a good joke! She
does not know what it is about. The cook finds the
story very funny, she insists. There is the table cov-
ered with books, notebooks and downstairs an amusing story: Lili does not choose the math homework,
she runs down the big wooden staircase. There they
are, downstairs: Rachel and Annie her little sisters,
Carole, her like-twin, Nicole the neighbor's daughter,
Lina the cook and... it would be only "them" if there
had not been the others! Lili sees them, Lili looks at
them! They must have been two or three. Maybe
two. In rags, timid, ready for anything and everything. The cook was watching them laughing, she had
already played that game, the plot was familiar. She
had already rehearsed the scene before the performance intended for the little girls. The others had to
play their parts to deserve the applause. They were
there insolent and terrified. They were hungry. The
child heard they were hungry when Lina gave the signal. She came out of the kitchen with leftovers that
she threw at them the way she threw bones at Pépé.
She threw the leftovers at them and they threw themselves over them. Then, she went back to the kitchen
and brought back the unwashed cauldrons, filled with
greasy and blackish water. They scraped the bottoms

and were still hungry. Even the trash cans? This was the promised farce! When there was nothing left, Lina kept on laughing and the little girls too, the little neighbor also, the little girl too was supposed to laugh, even though she did not know the end of the story. There was nothing else to give them and the woman said that they would eat anything: they nodded.

— Even bones?

— Yes, they said.

— Banana peelings?

— Yes, they said.

— The bottoms of trash cans?

— Yes, they said.

— Anything, laughed the one who no longer knew hunger.

Even the newspaper used to wrap the fish they swallowed laughing, it was the game, the reward for those who gave out of charity to their empty stomachs, earning the applause of the obliging public. It was important to amuse the good souls! They were eating this dirty and sticky newspaper, swallowing this printing ink. The story was as funny as the promise, much more than this math problem. The little girl disliked math, she preferred to have a good time.

ॐ

There was the math problem and there was the cook. The promise of an unequaled spectacle. One must not fear to tell it but in her conscience she already feels ashamed, the story is no longer this joke of the experienced moment. Difficult to recover it after the painful lesson. But it was also the lesson! Difficult to pretend writing, now, the little girl is waiting. No, she was waiting and watching the others. Difficult! Still, regrets are of no use. She found them funny. Are they still alive? The one who will not have the courage to hide the laughs, the one who, crying, will force the memory, despite her shame and rage, the one who by writing will force the cruel images to come out of the sealed drawers. Are they still alive? Those who because of hunger accepted anything, the leftovers, the trash, the newspaper, living on the learning dispensed by the written word, digesting in the most simple way this culture excluding them, are they still alive despite this unnatural food? Those who, in order to survive, seemed to have give up their dignity, have they learned to live? But, who had more dignity?

I learned about life near walls of grey concrete, turning around and around, top spinning out of control, in the space set by the law between buildings, looking for a bit of sky within my reach. I feel like running down dusty streets, dead trees burnt by the sun as far as the eyes can see. Weariness is breaking my bones. And I arrive, breathless at the big wooden house where those who died without a struggle are waiting for me. My weariness ebbs away for a moment. In my mind I go over the suicides' faces, blurred, eyes that do not see, lips dried out and on their cheeks a sign that I alone can decipher. I stay the whole day prostrate on the doorstep of the empty house, waiting for this army that has not risen up yet. I hear the muted cries of the living buried in the degrading routine, the screams of those who died without cause or reason and despite being defeated over and over again, I remain on the alert for the fast steps, the outstretched hands, the tight fists but the only perceptible noise is the tumult of my heart thrown into a panic. My temples are throbbing with fatigue. Pause. I spend a sleepless night, standing by the entrance of this cemetery of desires and passions. I no longer want to hear the silence and when I finally can close my eyes, their burning exhausts me. I collapse in front of this passage, endless void, waiting again for the aroused hordes with my arms extended and my patience spent, hoping for a courageous scream out in the open. I am waiting for our courage. I am waiting for my scream. And I am there, among them squatting in the wind, curled up inside myself, my hands are filled with rage and grip nothing. The soft light keeps me from seeing the new day, my shaking fingers and the bars which burn my back. There are dark places in my body where I no longer feel anything. Discouragement! I guard the entrance of my head against this crafty one, I stop the whirlwind and go back to life tiptoeing, for in a few hours I will lose my reflexes: the explosion is near.

But outside, it is nighttime, and in spite of my mad run, I hear another silence, the silence of my mother, and of the mother of my mother going back to the beginning of knowledge, to the age of the earth. Here and there, howling, screaming that nothing can muffle, sobs of those who had not a chance to make themselves heard, screams of horror of those who were giving birth to men forced to keep speaking and keep quiet these walled-up women. I can still hear the scream of the one whose muscles expelled me into the world of men, it stayed on my lips and my mouth is still open.

I continue and the silence of today no longer has the heaviness of old crosses. When my mouth closes for the night or for the kiss of my mother who is learning to speak, I know that elsewhere another one discovers the extent of her vocal cords. I fall asleep at peace, for one night forgetting the anxiety of the morrows, the sadness of knowing that I am too many to wear the gag, to keep the gag. One silence bogs me down, like the bars encircling an island imprison me for ever.

Story of a Day Like Any Other

Lili was walking along, repeating the same actions out of habit. She had so many times taken this road that she no longer noticed its details. A few meters on the left, making sure of the real absence of cars, crossing to the right because of the shade of the trees, accelerating at the circle where many cars cross, coming from four directions, four roads leading to the large square. The little girl was never afraid of this solo trip, four times a day because at noon she went home for lunch at the green house.

That morning, she was once again going through the daily motions. She had left early, in the morning the air smells so good. It did not take her much sweat to cross the large square, then she paused a long moment in front of the house with the white walls where, since her meeting with the man in black, she felt a tightening in her stomach. A few more meters before the shop of the Chinese man, then it would be the school crossroads. A few more meters when the noise made her jump. It is automatic, she looks toward the shop, pausing, the muffled sound seemed to come from there. She keeps walking slowly, hesitates in front of the shop, the little girl is surprised because usually the small room is full of people and noise. But it is in the street that the noise starts again and stops her in her tracks, looking at the woman, but it is no longer muffled like the first time. She realizes then, that it is coming from down below, near her school. A man comes out running, from the crossroads and, upon seeing her, without stopping shouts at her not to go on, to go back. The little girl knows that she is not allowed to skip school. She absolutely must go to school, besides such an idea would have never come to her mind, she loves going to school, she is a studious little girl. The good pupil walks on until the crossroads.

They are there, in the middle of the pavement, in front of the school; several men squatting behind a long car shoot at other men (who are the good guys and the bad guys in this anachronistic western?); the little girl saw them in a flash; eyes wide, standing, petrified in the sun, she hears a scream and someone pulls her away by the hand. The horror of this impression. She looked down toward a motionless body at her feet, she thought "a dead man" but the dead man turned his head toward her, stretched his arm out, pulling to him that little girl unaware of the danger. She falls against him, noticing the life in that stretched body. He holds her tightly, wanting to protect this unknown child. A few seconds, or minutes (in real time) or hours (of anguish) and it is silence, more terrifying than the previous noise. The man raises his head, still holding the child against him; slowly, he gets up, looks around the street, the house doors now closed, the schoolyard now deserted, after a while, he whispers to her to get up, begging her to keep her eyes shut. You must not see! She gets up, eyes open, sees all the dead bodies lying in the middle of the pavement, wants to go back, to go home and forget, but he takes her to school, knowing that the way home today is not safe for any little girl. He comforts her. It is over. Your parents will come and get you. She enters the schoolyard and rushes into her classroom. She has not asked him for his name, she has not thanked him. There was nothing to say. Later, no one will understand her friendliness with all the vendors of candies. Because of one image of candies scattered about on the sidewalk.

Of the rest of the day, praying with her teacher, crying with her friends, nothing will remain. She will only recall the long trips on foot when, every morning, her father will drive her to school.

∞

How does one recall events accurately? Is it so important to go on with the story? This young woman, writing a long time after, is striving for precision. Which one? That of dates and events lived or her own truth across the genesis of history? A long time after, can the events be retraced in their entirety? But she, leaning toward a past still near, cannot ignore this present that appears to be so far at times. She looks at herself and cannot believe the difference.

It's already been ten years. Ten years too many, too far or again too early. Ties cannot be undone by time or distance. That place sticks to her stomach beyond the snow, beyond life. To leave behind those years of restrained, repressed tears without rediscovering the indecent laughter? But did the tears exist? It matters little. When she remembers, there are tears, today's tears filling the absence of the tears that would not have been shed. And the rage to know. Nothing else can exist but pain. Only the right to suffer, without any possible choice, without escape; one does not forget the pain not to live, the pain to know that life is still impossible. Life, the possibility to laugh freely, the young woman refuses them. She thinks of herself as having no name, she no longer has a name, she is a young woman according to the dictionary. One must be identified with something, a word, to make a difference. She stays alone saying to herself words that no longer resonate. Magic of words which no longer resonate. And it is morning again. Which month was it? Which day?

It was early in the morning, early for that

country. The bullets no longer resonate. Did she hear the noise? Did she hear the enormous silence? Did she see this boy who heard her getting closer, moving forward in the middle of the silence? Did he extend his hand for her to lie down at his side in the middle of the pavement? Was he still holding her tight when they could no longer hear the bullets against the walls of the big school? Where did the bullets go that were no longer heard? The prayer under the class-room benches. Did she pray? To God or to the Devil? I salute you, full of hatred and screams, for the bullets that no longer resonate, for the bullets that are no longer heard rebounding. She will know later. She should have never known. She will know later that she will never be able to forget. She did not suspect that the sounds of the bullets would lodge themselves so deeply in her memory. Still, it was a time of dis-covery, of friendship, of the first emotions. It was a time when she should have been happy, protected by her lack of consciousness. But the memories will not be forgiving: she will forget the girls and boys, the fear of Paul's reaction at her inadequate results in mathematics. She will remember, with indulgence, her desire to die because of a zero in math. Her eager look at the speedy cars, her mute supplication to those cars racing along to run her over in order to avoid the reproaches of her father, to escape from her

91

own shame and she will laugh at her panic, at her tantrums of the little girl, at the tears shed without reason. If she laughs at everything, even if she makes fun of memories sometimes, she will never speak of this student bench under which she curled up, her ears trembling with the incessant noise of bullets which did not bounce.

I come out of it bruised, crying out for help to the one who cannot hear me. I have chosen to speak but cannot open my lips, I have opted for the scream but my eyes close as night gets near. To live a carefree life would be enough but once more I refuse to. How can I tell it? And why do you want me to tell?

This morning, I opened the book, images of him came back to my memory. I smiled at those smiles for which I shed tears to the very end, I told myself the beginning and my wish to destroy, I felt again the rage to survive the debacle? And I still have understood nothing. When do I stop looking for him among the new faces? Yesterday, his voice was soft and his stomach in a knot at the idea of no longer being able to let go of everything; the time before, he had been confronted with the unspeakable and forced to run away from it. I did not have the strength to accept his cynicism, his scorned pain. Without a word, without a gesture, paralyzed by a feeling of pride I was the only one to feel, I had started my life over. My former life.

Bursting out in fits of laughter, I see again the ocean, the forebearance, and the heritage of the sun. I had entrusted him with these images, I had given him the sand as a gift no longer wanting to use it, but I have taken everything back. Thunder belongs to me once more. I will swallow the wind to learn its anger. No, I did not forget anything, and I challenge those who took no decision to speak to me about the horror. The rage, I bear it tied up in knots in my stomach; it is swelling and the day of deliverance, I will laugh and give birth to a monster that I will tenderly rock and to whom I will sing the catastrophe. My fury will have been transmitted, the child will know how to destroy remorse and fear. I speak of misfortune in order to know. I scream my silence in order to learn how to speak and I am still muttering incoherent words, words whispered against the night, veiled words to forget mistrust. And you want me to tell you about love? I prefer the other stories because I will continue to ramble on until you fall asleep. And when, finally, I feel alone in the night, I will close my eyes to find again the little girl. Fast! Because there is little time left, she does not have much time before the coming of lucid understanding, last moments with the one who, within a summer, is about to grow up.

The Bookcase

Seated in the big armchair where Paul settled in every evening when the silence of the house let him read without interruptions, Lili was trying to find a solution to the problem which has been troubling her for an hour, since she overheard a conversation between Jeanne and the furtive stranger. She did not mean to listen, but neither one of the two speakers gave any attention to the quiet child playing at being afraid behind the big door of the living-room. And after the first sentences, she understood that the topic of this exchange did not concern her, but it was too late, the words pronounced nailed her to the ground.

— Is Doctor Michel home? I must see him to warn him of the danger.

Jeanne shook her head, Lili knew that she would not tell anything to this stranger, that she would let him talk, without stepping forth, cautious, as years of habit had taught her.

— You are Mrs. Paul? He remained standing up, visibly eager to end the conversation and leave. Shaking her head again, Jeanne kept silent.

— Mrs. Paul, please, warn the doctor that they are

conducting searches these days, that he should be careful to hide his books.

— I am sorry, sir, but my husband does not own any forbidden books.

The man looked at her, smiled, and left excusing himself for bothering her for nothing. Lili waited a moment, making sure Jeanne could no longer see her. Later, after leaving her involuntary hiding-place, she went to hang around Jeanne for additional information, hoping that Jeanne would tell her something or would call her father, but the woman went on with her work, apparently having already forgotten the incident. Thus, the child decided to act alone. She rushed to the office, and stayed in front of the bookcase for a moment, pausing, what could she do? She did not know which books the man alluded to. Then, after wracking her brain, a conversation with Paul came back to her.

It was during the Summer vacation. Lili, having exhausted her stock of books given to her for her birthday, went to find her father in order to get others. He was seated at his desk when she burst into the room.

— I want other books, I am tired of these baby stories, of the _Comtesse de Ségur_ and the _Club des Cinq_. Give me some of your books!

He had smiled.

— Come, let me explain! I am not against your taking my books, but not just any one. Look at this shelf, take a book, sit down, open it, read a few pages and tell me later if you want to continue. She will always remember, it was *The Little Prince*. She settled in the big armchair. It was nighttime when she looked up.

— It was wonderful! Why didn't you give it to me before?

— Because you never asked me before. All the books on   this shelf are yours now!

— And the others?

He smiled again, got up, walked toward her and taking her by the hand, led her in front of the bookcase.

— Take any one.

Her arm reached the third shelf, but she tried to reach the other books, stretching herself up to no avail on the tips of her feet to do it. Laughing, he caught her by the waist, lifted her up and she pulled a big book from the sixth shelf.

— Do the same thing, Lili. As soon as she read the first lines, she understood: *Le Paysan Haïtien* did not offer much to captivate even a curious little girl. Lili closed the volume and looked at her father who was observing her with a mocking smile.

— When you are tall enough to reach those books by yourself, you can read them. You are allowed to choose from the three shelves below, the others are forbidden not because I wish to hide anything from you, but because your arm is not long enough to reach these books! She still remembers Paul's laughter tickling her when she lifted her arm to try to reach even higher.

Seated in the armchair, she was looking at the shelves above, those with the forbidden books. Did Jeanne lie to the stranger? This bookcase had ten rows of books; if, for her, some were inaccessible, she calculated that even a very tall man could not reach the tenth row without a stool, where the forbidden books must be. The child got up and, trying to make as little noise as possible, balanced the armchair in front of the bookcase; then cautiously went up the makeshift scaffolding. One by one, she brought down the big volumes, that filled the last shelf and after thinking for a long time, went to hide them underneath the four mattresses of the little room. Her task done, she went down to find Jeanne. Her father had just arrived and the little girl, hearing the word book mentioned, announced proudly that she had fixed everything. To her astonished parents, she explained.

Jeanne was laughing; her father was smiling, looking at her with tenderness. He then explained to the anxious little girl that there was no reason for her to worry. There was no risk that the bogeymen would discover, in eventual searches, a forbidden book because there had never been any, in the library, or then all of them were forbidden and that the four mattresses would not be enough. The child did not understand Jeanne's laughter for she thought the difficult times had returned, nor the explanations of the father which in fact explained nothing.

— Not The Little Prince, surely not!

— And why not? St-Exupéry did have the little prince say, "I am responsible for my rose!" You understand, of course, that forbidden books contain something else but I am trying to explain to you that all censure is arbitrary. The Inquisition burned the books that stated the Earth was round, when for you such a statement seems evident. To censure is to forbid, to destroy everything that is different, contrary to established principles, to the rules. The books on the tenth shelf are my study-books, the ones that I rarely use, the others are in my clinic!

Lili was not sure to have correctly understood, but every summer, she extended her arm, hoping her hand would be able to reach the fourth shelf. She was in a hurry to grow up.

∾

From where do these images of light and darkness come? She will never know with certainty. In spite of everything, she often tries to recapture, once she has identified the faces after the return of events that she thought lost, the word, the gesture or the object that brought back this moment not-chosen from the bottom of the drawer. The one who dreams in the night has sometimes no difficulty finding the trigger. On a sunny but cold February afternoon, a little room where a few people, most often alone, adopt the same position, erect, staring at the screen, every once in a while making an instinctive gesture to avoid getting stiff. *Fahrenheit 451* on the screen, she sees books being burned and from far back, returns the anguish of a little girl seated in an armchair, trying to avoid the imminent catastrophe.

She finds the trigger and is surprised at the ease with which these images impose themselves, without fear or pain. Why is it that at other times the words do not come to her with such serenity?

I am here, screaming, wounded by this pain in my stomach, neither too strong, nor too well located, a dull and steady pain coursing through my body stopping nowhere, resting nowhere, settling nowhere, melting away, flowing through me like a burning and freezing wave. I do not want to describe this madness; I do not want to describe this scream I feel slowly growing from the top of my head of mad woman to the tips of my far-away toes scoffing at me. I want to write for Maya, tender, lilac tales, sweetness and calm. But hatred and fear turn around my legs tied up. Lucie says: "You are surrounded by a lilac-colored halo, not exactly lilac but in the hues you love so much, the colors of the salon rue Sherbrooke, blending in this halo that shines around you. And sometimes yellow.... Tender is this color, altruistic!" I do not want to listen to the scream. Tenderness, says Lucie. I want tenderness for Maya, I want the tenderness of the tales that sing of anything, in order not to scream, and I tell stories of calm seas. Everything is so far, too far, I do not succeed in finding the real smells, the taste of my tears, the sincerity of my hatred. I detest my childhood and its sealed drawers. I detest my non-memory. I can only remember these images, yellowed postcards, misplaced slides, frozen images, with their frozen insipid smiles. Where to look? Where to find what announced this madness? The photograph of this traveler above the table (a yellow dining-room, its chairs padded with thick yellow fabric, its yellow curtains, and, on a yellow wall, a photo in a brown frame) near which Jacques and Marie attempt to feed me. He is there, opposite my chair, I keep in my mouth the food I refuse to swallow, that swells my cheek one bite a minute until the shapeless heap oozes out, drips down from the left corner of my mouth and melts away on the white linen dress. I always found something to do during the time of non-hunger. Marie was forced to say, one tearful day, "His name is Alexandre," the rest of the story will come later.

Eli, cynical, answers me. He did not come to help anyone. He wanted to defend his own interests and his clan's. I truly want to listen to reason, my love, I am willing to wipe the slate clean of my legend but can you tell me whether his death does not deserve a certain indulgence? Can you tell me why I should not have the right to cry for the traveler, when as a little girl, listening to the noise of bullets, I persisted in dreaming of hope? This photo of the traveler is a lesson in pain. And I tell him: if pain was not there, why write? Pain everywhere, pain in everything. Do you see me writing about the happy days? Only the days of happiness, fresh breeze, tenderness, sunshine? Why write about the passing of quiet days when everything should be beautiful, without fear of the morrows, without the anguish of empty stomachs, without the screams of the tortured, without the empty sockets of the zombified? Without hatred and rage, why lose my time endlessly writing? In my head the dreadful admission: if the fear was not there, why write? I have read the very first pages over and only kept the pain of surviving. I was sincere, I wanted to be honest. I have described to you the few hours of full sun, I have described to you the seconds of serene love, I have invented for you a livable world. Do you remember "a world where happiness..." this text that you alone know in its first version because I have transformed it. I could no longer stand those incantatory dreams. I hated my impulse to write about the happy days to come, without ever succeeding in keeping the tone. There had to be death, tearing, fear sticking to the body or at least the days of inertia, stupor, the long years of numbness. Today, I have set aside those blue pages. Because of my writing style, I said. A pretext perhaps. Why choose the words that relate the sad story? When I saw blue pages again, the blue like a clear sky, nothing but the red pages, red like blood, seemed true to me. If it was not for the blood of capital punishment in the very center of the city, in front of schoolchildren dragged there by educators haunted by the need to survive, all pedagogy abolished by the horror, why spend all those nights, dead tired, tracing these letters?

As for Paul, he had faced his fear, challenged the law, and kept his daughter home. There was no television set in the green house, for everything was on television. And yet, she remembers.

You are a virtuous adult. You landed in this country by accident. It must be by accident. Who would, out of his own free will, get stuck here? Especially not you, a conscious, responsible adult. Imagine a forced landing, an unplanned stop. And there you are in this foreign country. You knew about this island, about the distant reality of this old French colony, you are a well-informed adult. It is eight o'clock in the morning and you find yourself walking in the streets of that city. A long day to spend in this dirty and foul-smelling city. The heat of the tropics, the flies glued to the piles of rubbish right in the middle of the cracked streets full of potholes. That reality makes you want to throw up. You would have liked to feel indulgent, but the filth, the misery, the rags, the swollen stomachs assault you. To run away, or at least escape from these downtown streets, to go toward the clean neighborhoods with flowers everywhere. In every city, there are clean neighborhoods with flowers everywhere, especially in a capital city! You know that here just a few hundred meters away are enough for you to shut your eyes on the intolerable reality. You ask for information. Those people around you understand more or less your language. A determined young man starts the dialogue. You say "beautiful neighborhoods," he understands. You want to be sure "pretty flowers, public squares," in his eyes you saw he understands. He asks if you would like to have a guide. You accept his presence because you feel you can put up with his cheerful face (not happy, but cheerful, you thought!). His clothes seem clean and he is visibly not a beggar. You follow him in the heat, the crowd, the mud and the extended hands. After walking a few minutes, you finally get to a place where the air becomes bearable. You are feeling much better and continue this heartening tour walking slowly. Your companion tries at times to speak to you, you try to do the same. Through words, gestures, you show your pleasure. Next, he leads you to the large square: leafy trees, a water fountain, benches in the shade, you discover a different city. People walk by or cross you but your presence among them does not seem out of place and you forget also the anomaly of your sightseeing visit looking at these flower gardens smelling of jasmine and camellia. Your guide makes a suggestion. You think he wishes to show you the local attractions. His kindness stops you, you fear the places reserved for disenchanted tourists, but you accept. He signals you to hail a taxi, a line as they say. You climb into the old car while your companion indicates to the driver a destination you prefer to ignore. You watch the streets, the houses you go by, appreciating the sudden changes with the neighborhoods you cross when, suddenly, the car stops; you step down and realize you are at the gates of a cemetery. You want to object but the guide signals you to follow him. Besides, you see a lot of people crowding at the gates of this sinister place. You wonder what could attract them there, what ceremony is about to take place behind those walls. You go inside.

1967, that year will remain engraved somewhere in your mind. You think you had forgotten but with certain images you recall the intolerable sensation, and the events of that day of sightseeing flash by in front of your eyes: the cemetery gate you enter, preceded and followed by a great number of people, your generous guide, his youth and his winning smile, the tombs big and small, white or with glaring colors under the sun of that country where you came in spite of yourself, by accident. The clamminess and the sweat trickling down your neck, wetting your clothes, so many sensations which will never fail to take you back to that day and that place. You see again those schoolchildren identifiable by their uniforms. You remember thinking "but what are all these children doing here?" You thought at the time that there was going to be a ceremony for the funeral of a local celebrity (a famous writer, a decorated educator, a political man?) and you decided to ask the young man what was the reason for all these people to come to that place. His evasive answer did not seem strange: "They have been summoned, everyone has been summoned". You suspected nothing yet at the sight of these men in uniform that the young guide pointed out to you, you only chose to imagine the burial of a political man. When you arrived to the place where all the others stopped, you did not understand why, in the middle of that empty space, there were two poles erected under the sun.

About that stay so short in a country that was heretofore unknown to you, you have never talked. Or so little. You have only talked about the sun and a malaise. On the boat or on the plane, you had to explain to your companions your distraught looks, and you mentioned nausea, vomiting because of the sun. A sunstroke, you explained. You already wanted to forget that having entered a cemetery without knowing why you had witnessed, along with a large crowd of adults and children, the execution of two guerillas. All the same, in front of certain images, in a newspaper or on television, you experience the same unbearable sensation.

That story is part of my usual nightmares. I am at the same time the hallucinating foreigner, the smiling guide and the little girl sitting motionless on her bed throughout that day. She had had the opportunity to be left out, he had been reckless enough to keep her at home, in spite of the convocation.

That story is part of my nightmares. And yours. I was at the age of the first lessons. I did not know the name of the man who, the ritual over, gave the two men the coup de grâce. Do they still say coup de grâce? You knew his name and his face and you had told me about the horror of that journey a mere centimeters away from him, everything in you recoiled at being actually so close to him but there was nothing you could do. To your nightmares was added the haunting presence of the executioner you had been in contact with. Some nights you were in turn each one of these individuals, including the two men that the little girl will later see on glossy paper. Because of that photograph, because of these nightmares, violence suffuses your calm face.

Beyond the logic of the arguments learned and renamed the scientific theory of history, I still keep my secret wishes, my crazy, big girl's wishes which I learn to spell with sociology, economics, philosophy and history books, dry books which I often fail to understand. Cruel, you make fun of me, and I want to be cynical. The desire for revenge is long-lasting. If it is not because of the pain, she writes, why write? The pain of an intellectual. My head hurts. I am hungry in my head, I have suffered all the tortures in my head, because of those who are hungry, hurting, for those suffering from malnutrition, illiteracy, for those who go barefoot, in rags, for those with the highest rate of infant mortality, for those with a forty year life expectancy, for those executed in the public square or in the silence of anonymity; if it is not for the daily horror of those people, why write? And, yet, you say, everywhere, you are not writing for them.

The Rocking-Chair

Those were the last moments. She thought she had gone around the circle of joy, tasted all that emotions and dreams could concede to that quiet girl. Paul had grown up and nothing could pierce her indifference. She faintly smiled when they teased her about her boyfriends, a long line of forgotten faces that she slipped into a picture album to rediscover, later on, their blurred features if not their names. Her lips did not move when they talked about her academic success, what are your plans for the future, my darling? For she concealed her desires, even the reasonable choices. She would slightly open her eyes when they talked about her coldness, her detachment. And, they were astonished by her bursts of laughter when they gave the rocking-chair as a proof of her irresponsibility, indifference and recklessness.

She loved that rocking-chair and on the day when the boat shot missiles (one fell in the courtyard of the green house damaging a window of the second floor), she was gently rocking and humming, stopping after each explosion to say "one," "two," "three," that one must have fallen in the large square "four," listen, it sounds as if it has exploded in the courtyard. I should go and see. She had gone and looked while the others were hastily throwing a few clothes into a suitcase, then taking her by the arm, dragged her with them. They were not more afraid than she was. She was not more courageous. I cannot accept erroneous interpretations here. They, telling later about the rocking-chair, will mention her indifference; she will say nothing. It was neither awareness, nor courage, nor coldness, nor indifference. It was the routine of one who knew nothing else, the indolence of a girl judging it a waste of time to have to find, after each storm, the saving fear, the instinct for survival.

The last time, there will be tenderness. Of that day, she will keep the pleasure of laughing and the sweetness of the heart that beats. Paul arrived at school very early. Since the incident of the flag that had made her cry so much, she had convinced herself that it was preferable to hold on to her distant and polite mask, showing any sign of the joy to breathe was profane. Her dreams were the stupidities of a little girl. She had never revealed to them her greatest passion. She would say, in secret, "One day, I will fly a plane," and the reason of what they called madness, recklessness was her passion for flying.

As usual, everything had started with a familiar noise that her brain refused to identify. The grown-ups, upon hearing it, said nothing. She, defying fate, persisted in crying out, "Listen, a flat tire." Sometimes, the flat stayed isolated and silence buried the questions but that time she repeated the sentence like an incantation.

— Martin, did you hear? A tire just exploded.

At the second one:

— Listen, Martin, another tire!

— The fourth time, he loses his temper.

— Be quiet, you very well know that it is not a succession of flat tires, for goodness sake!

The teacher is looking severely at them. He was desperately trying to dissipate the fear and pretend he had heard nothing. A girl in the next classroom starts screaming. The scream rings like a signal. The teacher gets up still looking dignified and goes out through the large back door after having asked them to stay inside. Martin looks at her, worried by her impish smile.

— Come Martin, let's go see what is going on.

— You are crazy, we must not move!

— Come on! First let's find Rachel and pick up Annie, next to see what's going on!

She goes out into the large courtyard already

deserted, he follows her grumbling. While opening the doorway of the lower school, to the younger children, she hears the first volleys. The noise is getting closer. Against the loud background, another noise, a whirring, followed from time to time by another explosion. Annie was waiting for her. She drags her toward the other building, tells Carole, on her way, to keep the little ones in the upper student classroom and asks her to go check that Rachel is safe in the library. All three of them rush toward the large room. They arrive in time to see the English teacher entering it and pulling shut the heavy doors behind him. They slip in.

— Why are you shutting the door, Miss, he asks?

— Some of them are across the street, on the balcony of the house close by and they have shot in our direction. As if to prove her right, shots are heard against the heavy iron doors. One of the boys starts to cry, the teacher rushes to him. Far away again, the whirring.

— Annie, stay here with Martin, I am coming right back.

— Lili, you can't....

But she goes out after having slightly opened one side of the door and looked outside. Silence. She hugs the wall all the way to the stairway. She knows the way; during recess or the noon break, she often dragged Martin toward that stairway that ended at a small iron door which blocked the access to this forbidden area, the concrete roof. She had found a way to force the lock, and at high noon when half the school children had left, she made herself comfortable high up at the top to look down at the city. She would sit in the shade of the house next door, praying to the heavens that no passers-by lift their heads and recognize the school uniform. In spite of the commotion of the moment, she is convinced that no one can catch her. In all likelihood, her absence will not be noticed; in the confusion and the panic, several students had changed classrooms looking for the security of familiar faces. In front of the little door, Lili hesitates, afraid of being let down by what she is about to observe from the top of her lair. But, she goes on to the place where she flattens herself down in the narrow shade, surprised by this shrunken space until she understands why: she usually went to the roof at noontime and the sun was not in the same place. She had been lying down for a few minutes when the crackling started again. They were settled on the balcony of the house that gave shade. She hears their muffled exclamations and it is the shout of a man that attracts her attention to the explosion fast followed by the whirring of a plane getting closer. Lili looks to the north. The crackling noise intensifies. Paul, lying down, sees the dark point getting closer. The noise of the plane is getting as loud as that of a submachine gun. She watches. When the plane is but a few meters away from the school, she gets up, crouches, leaning against the wall. She waits. It is getting closer and its noise little by little drowns the noise of the guns. They are getting closer. She can see them. The plane is very close. For a few seconds, she is but eyes and pounding heart. They are two of them: the pilot and another one, stripped to the waist, wearing khaki-colored shorts, one leg hanging out of the small plane with its door open. He has one leg out and through the window she sees his face. Clasping her hands, she looks at the man on the plane, the man and the plane, and the one who is not the pilot fascinates her. The apparatus flies past the school and does an about-turn over the bay. She does not move. During the long minutes separating both passages, she does not move, motionless, in the shade of the wall, crouched, hands clasped, eyes closed, waiting for the whirring which will cover the crackling of the bullets. She had decided, while waiting, to stay there the whole day if necessary, watching them fly over. Even the entire night. But the second time they fly over, there is the look from the other one. She smiles and the other one looks at this child-pupil hidden in the shade of the gunmen. The other one looks, horrified, and she gets scared. The other one, who, for a fraction of a second, could guide the look of these men lying in ambush on the balcony of the house. She flattens herself even more on the floor and listens to the sudden silence of the guns. Then, she creeps along to the small iron door and goes into the opening. Shielded, she looks one last time at the plane heading toward the sea and runs down the stairs. She will never know whether this glance was directed at her, that man was perhaps staring at something else, elsewhere or at someone else. But he forced her to climb back down toward Annie's tears, Martin's anger and the noise of the bullets against the heavy iron doors.

From the years of understanding, she will remember much. But the most bruising events will linger on the surface of her memories. The first injustice, the first personal scar of a broken system of values. And Martin... they are both in the back of the truck, furious because of the unexplained tardiness of the others even though they had agreed upon the time. They were supposed to leave the city before 7:30 to avoid the scorching heat during the trip, to take advantage to the maximum of that day by the seaside. And the others who are not showing up! The young girl jumps off into the street. He follows her, without worrying about the basket containing swimsuits and sandwiches. Both of them, barefoot on the sidewalk, observe the street one way then the other. Nothing. After a while, Marthe arrives. There had been a misunderstanding. The others are waiting in the courtyard, across from the classroom, their meeting place. It is the first day of vacation. To study. They are big now. Soon the official exams. They are learning to be responsible for their time. Paul runs off to get the others. Martin follows. It is 7:45 a.m. In the middle of the large courtyard, those who stay at school are assembled, students, teachers, director, for the morning salute to the flag. They know the rules. Paul and Martin stop, breathless, waiting for it to end. One pair of eyes. Two pairs of eyes. The singing is over. A hand signal. He looks at her. You? Him to her. No, you. Both of you. But what do they want? They wanted an exemplary punishment. You are monsters. Even worse. Daring to insult your flag. Presenting yourselves half-naked, barefoot, in order to show your hostility. They were threatening. Neither child understood. The intervention of a teacher will be needed to avoid the expulsion. They will never understand this outburst of anger. They will never understand whom they wanted to punish. In what way could their bare feet be an insult to the flag? The majority of the people in our country walk about barefoot, for lack of shoes. Is it an insult to the flag?

Silence all around!... I woke up filled with anguish at the recurrent nightmares that go on, in a strange continuation of identical dreams. For years, I had dreamed about another world; always at the times I had questions, I would get back in the cycle; from elsewhere, coming from an indeterminate place, a being showed me the way bringing me the elements of the solution. Under several forms, with variants in places and methods, several nights in a row for many weeks, I would dream the same theme: I had in my hands, due to the generosity of the one coming from very far, what was needed to find a solution. I would wake up with a strange, contradictory feeling; joy at having been able to do it, frustration for owing this joy to someone else. Now, the anguish! The theme has changed: the one coming from elsewhere no longer allows me to access to knowledge, he takes away from me all autonomy, makes me suffer while trying to help me. Last night, it was about a forced exile. The others were leading me, along with people I love, to their world, in order to take us away from the unbearable; and after the first moment of discovery and wonder, feeling like a captive in the midst of all this perfection, I try to run away and go home. Why this flight? In the morning, a sensation of anguish overcomes me...

Upon recalling certain texts in my drawers, I notice the reverse of the usual phenomenon. The former dreams, so intense, so often repeated, I had transformed into writings. And so among other texts, I know I can find a forgotten story that I just recognized, upon waking up: my nightmares written beforehand. Have I already lived these hallucinations?

And the Days of Sadness...

The years had gone by with hours of difficulty, dull days and a few seconds of happiness. Lili had grown up some more and was still as plain. When she looked at herself in the mirror of the big wardrobe, studying her insignificant face, her legs too long, her arms too skinny, the pronounced curve of her buttocks and everywhere her muscles of a little dancer, she kept a critical mind. Lucid, having decided once and for all not to suffer from her appearance which could not be changed and with which she would spend the rest of her life, accustomed to her plainness, even thinking about it with tenderness. At least I will not be loved for my attractive looks! She did not even dare think because I am beautiful, this word seemed sacrilegious when applied to her. Only her bust found grace in her eyes! She had always felt that since no part of her body mattered to her, Mother Nature could do whatever it wanted, but from the very beginning of puberty, Lili had repeated like an incantation, to a distant and unnamed divinity, please do not let them grow, I pray you, please do not let me have a big bust. Her wish had been granted perhaps, because, being a sensible girl, she only had one wish. She had made it her duty to listen attentively; giving the appearance of someone who, having listened, would put in practice all the advice that the older girls would give her: Stand up tall! Do not walk bent over! Your breasts will sag! Exercise! She often repeated these recommendations, stand up tall, and she would walk, thrusting her shoulders forward to conceal her small bust, and in the same manner with every other piece of advice that she would use the other way round. And during the days of sadness, Lili will recall her wishes and, like a prayer, will whisper, "Thank you for having made me plain!"

Nothing was going well at the green house. It had started with Martin. In addition to his daily visits after school, to study together, to laugh or rehearse their naughty tricks, he often stayed for a long time at Lili's where he felt at home and Paul would tease him, saying that he had had no difficulty raising this son he was very proud of..

One afternoon, she waited for Martin for over an hour, in vain, and in the end, tired, she decided to go home alone to the green house. He came around six o'clock, his clothes torn, his face swollen refusing to answer his friend's questions. Paul called him then and they shut themselves in the library where they stayed by themselves for a long time; when they came out, Martin still looked tense. He left without having spoken to his friend. She then questioned her father. Martin had fought with another schoolboy who had alluded to Marcel's situation, to his father. He did not elaborate, she had understood. She knew the story, these facts had been known to her for such a long time! And if in Martin's room the photograph of a young woman watched over his sleep, he had never talked about her to Lili, about that mother who, a long time ago, during some vacation in Jérémie, had not returned home, and if no one had had any news of her, everyone knew that the bogeymen would never give her back. Martin had been left alone with his father.

Then years had gone by. At first Marcel had refused to believe that he would never see her again, and one day, he had met a woman and started to love her. Martin also, in spite of the memories of the happy days with this mother who would never return home, had understood and he wanted his father to find happiness again, a sunny happiness different from all these sordid adventures he guessed in spite of the man's discretion. He was, after all, the first one to speak of marriage, knowing just like Marcel and Raymonde that a life together would be difficult outside this frame. Marcel started the process, gathered information on the formalities to consider and the answer came, brutal, even though it was suggested by a friend who had his best interest at heart: he had to ask for a divorce for desertion of the conjugal home, drag Claire's name in the mud, deny their happiness and these ten years' pain, clear the name of the bogeymen. He refused and unhappy Martin was fighting against stupidity and ignorance. Lili felt bad, recalling their joy at the idea of the preparations, their games in front of the mirror of the wardrobe when, he stiff and she moved, mimicked the yes and the fainting of the young bride.

The next day, he did not come to school. When on his return, three days later, Lili placed her hand on his arm to show him she understood, he looked at her and simply said: "I need to do sports and get strong; when my little sister is born, I will break the jaws of all those who will allude to her situation." That same week, Marthe tried to kill herself by drinking all the drugs she found in the bathroom cabinet of her parents' big, luxurious house. At the hospital, she had told Lili that her father wanted her to get engaged to an awful man whose status as a bogeyman was a secret to no one. And Lili saw in her friend's eyes that she was beginning to wonder about her father.

She was crying, during those days of sadness, over her two friends that she could not help, whose sadness could be not eased through words. And in her head, secretly saying "Claire was too beautiful, Marthe is too beautiful, thank you for making me plain!" She still had not grasped it all.

Thank you for making me plain! She holds no rancor toward that child convinced that her plainness would drive danger away. And she will remember words, when, confronting their bad faith, she tried to explain the other misunderstanding. She has been raped because she was beautiful, because she wore too short a skirt, because of her manners, because.... The woman knows the little girl was wrong, beauty did not explain anything, being ugly would not have been in any way a protection. Violence whatever its form is always aimed at the weakest. Martin understood. The woman knew now what Lili still ignored, the important thing is not to be ugly but to become strong.

I had forgotten the extent of their malice even though I know them. But the beginning of my retreat, away from their sterile words, their feverish agitation and hypocritical fraternity, had made me forget the unhealthy power of their speeches. They wanted to hurt me, deliberately, there had been a brief look of pleasure in their eyes. I had escaped from them before it was too late, they have never forgiven my lucid lucky star. Eli says that they were able to get at me but he does not understand the reasons for my sadness. Angry at first about their false concern, only feeling sadness because they had not affected me, I made the void around me. Sadness because of second-hand information, provided to create the setting, to illustrate their usual distance, not knowing they will be the only words I would recall; as for the rest, Paul, the slander, their cynical sweetness oozing the "they pretend that...", all that was going on far away from me. I know Paul, in spite of the time, in spite of the distance, I know false any report of compromise, even of arrangements, Paul will never compromise with anyone.

The innocent reference to Marthe, (it was lucky they did not know we were old friends and even if they had known, they would not have understood its importance) made accidentally at that time, felt like a slap already received. The name of Marthe shook me, the words they said accused little Lili of being an incurable idealist. Eli thinks the little girl must be absolved, that she was moreover defending an acceptable principle. In theory! I have not been able to forgive him. Pride, says he, you refuse the mistake in the case of Marthe, but think of the other examples. I accept everything although the arguments, the vehemence of the little girl trouble me. "You are being unfair, you do not have the right to judge in this way, it is not because Marthe is the daughter of a bogeyman that she cannot be decent, I am sure that she is not aware of her father's actions and that if she discovered them, I know she would condemn them. Marthe did not do anything, why do you want me to hold her responsible for the evil actions of someone else? Give her a chance, do not be so intransigent, see how much she appreciates our way of life, in spite of her father's interdictions, she stood her ground, she wants to remain my friend. Don't be as stupid as he is." The little girl desperately argued, with other words perhaps, but moved by the same feelings. I would argue until I was blue in the face and Paul's sadness seemed to me the worst insult. I could have braved his anger, his own defense mechanism but this sadness drove me away from a world, from a truth he alone possessed! I was angry with him, I am still angry with him that he knew before I did that Marthe would choose. You are exaggerating, says Eli. Put aside your damn pride! You knew a long time ago that Marthe had made her choice. What is the date of your last letter? And even at that time, weren't you already using a detached and *superficial tone for this semblance of correspondence. He is right, I had already accepted it. I had accepted even more. Eli you know it! In theory only, there is the flaw! How many times have we not discussed what would happen if one of us would jump over the fence, if one of us turned away from our mutual choice? And the painful consequences? How many times, exorcisms, have we tried to guess who would suffer the most? If it is me, it will change nothing in my love, but you, on the other hand, would not be able to love a different man, different since no longer thinking like the Eli you know. No, you would detest that unchanged woman whose choices would be reprehensible to the person you will have become. And again my turn. And again yours. It had become a game, cruel and reassuring, each of us looking for the weakness of the other, the words which would say in any possible way I will always love you and the sigh when neither of us slipped. Words, Eli, intellectual thoughts about potential outcomes that, deep down, we do not believe in, discussions possible because of our self-confidence. You may be right, it must be arrogance. I could not stand it that he would put Marthe in that category. He answered back using the other category, me Paul, daughter of Paul, a close relative of the dead traveler and he was right. In spite of the aggressiveness of my arguments, I have not changed. I said, that, like for Marthe, it was an accident of birth, I had wanted to forget the little girl's looks,*

Paul's words explaining the forty days, the loneliness creating between us an understanding where the age difference was no longer important. Paul was telling me how difficult it is to maintain a friendship with those who are demanding, he was demanding and in the green house, we were almost always alone. When, for a while, a face appeared, two faces, these people I observed, who deserved a beginning of attention, very quickly disappeared. Paul then explained the disappointment and we would end up alone once more. At other times, in the evening, he would drive us to our grandmother's; we knew then that he and Jeanne were going out to try and have a good time. But these precious evenings seemed to us too few. It's not easy for those who are demanding to have a good time.

Where Mr. Bell Comes on Stage and Is Declared Guilty by the Society of Righteous Adults

Once upon a time, there were two, three, four or even more phone conversations between those strange people who discovered that they could laugh. Everything began one Tuesday afternoon at four o'clock, and she thought this story would never end. She already knew him, she had seen him at different times during her brief visits at the clinic. He had just completed his years of residency and Paul had accepted him at his side to gain some experience until the young man went abroad to specialize as he wanted to. On that day, she wanted to win a bet, to know whether it was true that he displayed calmness and understanding toward his patients, any patient, as directed by his profession. In reality, she wished to make him drop his impeccable professional demeanor. She knew Paul was away and asked the secretary to put her through to his substitute.

— Hello, I would like to make an appointment for tomorrow afternoon.

— Of course. What is your name?

— Patricia Louis. She said Patricia and he believed her. Her name was still Paul and every one kept calling her Lili, still on that day around four o'clock, she claims her name is Patricia, this was part of the plan. She chooses to be Patricia, to avoid the questions and the inevitable silence, the cold politeness, the smiles addressed elsewhere. Paul did not expect to keep the game going. The next day, before the time agreed for the appointment, she is still Patricia.

— I apologize but I cannot make the appointment.

Once again, she makes an appointment for the next day and, then, that Thursday, cancels it once more.

— I am really confused...

— I understand. Do you want to come tomorrow? I ...

— No, I would prefer Monday.

— I am sorry, I cannot take your name down today. Please, call back tomorrow.

She calls back, teasing.

— It's still me Patricia!

— He speaks once more calm, polite. And after...

— Do not hang up. There is a problem. We need to talk.

She holds the line. When he returns, she senses the preoccupation of the doctor; he asks her how she feels, and why she wanted a consultation, Lili then confesses the deception.

— I am sorry, I was pulling your leg. I am not sick, I only wanted to meet you! Are you angry?

He wasn't. Between two consultations, between two calls, they open up to each other. Patricia liked the sound of that strange voice or a speech impediment, little did it matter to the girl who was discovering the difference.

— Good morning Patricia! I would like to meet you.

She gets used to this name, she no longer hesitates when he pronounces it, but the request worries her, bringing her back to a reality that the game had until then masked. A pleasant mystery, she imagined herself beautiful–imprisoned–by-evil-being-waiting-for-courageous-friend-ready-to face-for-her-sake-any-peril.

— I would like to but it is difficult. I have two brothers who do not let me go out alone.

The lie is enormous but he believes her because she is Patricia. There must always be men to lock up a woman, she invents two jealous brothers to go on with the story. And they chat about little nothings and big nothings, they learn to laugh together and soon the voice is no longer enough.

— Don't you want to meet me?

— Yes, of course, but...

— Try to make an effort!

Patricia replies:

— I will come tomorrow. No, Tuesday. I will have a red shirt on, you will be able to recognize me.

On Tuesday, she wears this large blue shirt that fits her so badly and in which she feels so comfortable. She speaks to him, he looks at her without seeing her, on the look out for all the girls walking by, jumping at each piece of red fabric on bodies that never walk up to him.

— You did not come!

— Yes, I did and I spoke to you but I was not wearing a red shirt!

She reveals the lie, now useless, she is not Patricia, she tries again the game "guess who I am" and she screams with laughter. She cannot bring her-self to tell him, not because she finds her name ugly, not because her name is Paul or because she is called

Lili, what is the importance of one more name? She would have told him on the first day, my name is Paul if there was not another obstacle. She cannot bring herself, despite the distance provided by the telephone, to confess; she gives a reference. He understands: the daughter of the other one. And there is silence, there was nothing to explain, he is going to accept or hang up. He must be asking himself if she is fooling around. Does truth lie in the difference of a name? It is not about the other one! He suddenly recovers the sound of his voice, that voice so often heard when Lili was calling the other one, he says he remembers her face and the fragility of the back of her neck. When, lucid, she will say that she is ugly, he will talk about the fragile neck he caught a glimpse of, one dull theater evening. He does not hang up. Muffled voices, broken sentences, she feels his malaise. Has the complicity of anonymity been lost? There was no anonymity, she was still herself, she had been herself under the name of Patricia, truthful in her lie. As for him he thought he had been speaking to a stranger and she was the daughter of the other, of his boss. It's not about the other one. Is he thinking about the words pronounced without reserve, about the stories told to Patricia, that he would not have said to the daughter of the other one or was he thinking about all those who would doubt the sincerity of his affection for the daughter of the big boss? Silence, it is not about the other one. Worry too, and in her head, obstinate and torn, she demands trust. Given to the end of memory! With their first laugh together while Patricia's shadow melts away with their first look, the other one disappears, they have pulled down the wall. For her it will be the first step towards change. They will learn to foil the compulsory silence when, surrounded by all those hostile faces, spying upon their smiles, they will have to express everything with a gesture of the hand. The young girl lets herself be taken over by the excitement of the moment, these exams that must decide her future, the study period with her friends, the possibility of seeing him because of the independence newly acquired. Furtive meetings, she does not feel she is cheating, the others are the ones who cheat. She does not cheat when she confesses her discovery, when she reveals her fear to him. Not because of some moral standards or prejudice! She wanted to discover it all with him. Tenderness. Complicity. Also pleasure, but her body balks, her body refuses when her head has already granted all. She can no longer stand the forced secrecy, the room of a friend where she jumps at every sound of footsteps on the stairway. She refuses to learn pleasure on the run, she wants to be in the broad daylight in his arms and prefers to wait.

One day, at Martin's house, they enter the sitting-room that the light of the sun does not reach. A dark room with an awful couch. She sees nothing, only her brain registers: she is wearing a pleated skirt and the blue shirt, he a brown pair of pants. He often wears dark colored clothes. He offers her books, an anthology by a poet, his friend, and by Eluard "political poems," "love and poetry" to court a still little girl, to open the barrier, to bring down the barricade of fear. She knows that with him she does not have to censure her words, to hide her anger, to mask her intuitions. She tells him everything. And it is the sharing of memories, fits of laughter with the girlfriends, exercises of seduction, pain of knowing, of having discovered too early her consciousness. She talks about her discussions with Paul, the first lessons, her rebellion at Jocelyne's departure, her favorite friend. Older than her. Her best friends were all a few years older. Jocelyne, too pretty, reckless, who had not understood the danger in pleasing that man. When he insisted, she refused to meet him, spoke to Lili about him. Secret talks with Paul. Hurried meetings of the parents who then felt the storm coming. The bogeyman was getting impatient, wanted to speak seriously. Then one morning, Paul waited in vain for her friend. She felt that departure like a failure, this feeling spoiling her own plans because it was also time for her to

leave. He knows it. He, too, will have to leave short-
ly after, to a different country from hers. They swear
to each other to do everything possible to be together
afterward. They discuss innumerous meetings.
Indecisive, she does not know whether this trip is a
good thing. She would have wished for another country, another choice but Julia is waiting. Julia, seen
three years earlier during a first trip, Julia who had
had to leave her country, her friends, because she and
Fred could no longer stand it. They, too, like
Jocelyne, left in sandals, without luggage so as not to
attract any attention. They too pretended to be at the
airport, to accompany someone, and at the last
minute, without saying goodbye, walked to the plane
as if they were not afraid. Departures. And it is their
last meeting. She wants to say to him more words, to
hold on to the tears but her voice breaks and her smile
is nothing but a wet grimace. She believes then that
the wish to leave is tied to the promise to be with
Michel next summer, in New York, for the tenderness of long talks, for the joy to laugh out loud, to
creep in broad daylight in a great bed. In spite of
everything, it is painful to leave.

৵৵

The pain that takes over. Drowned. The
sweetness of being which does not end. A little girl
does not succeed in establishing well-defined bound-

aries. Safe borders and safeguards. Later. It will be too late. Here, there, everything is cushioned, blurred, warm. It is not sufficient to decide happiness in the past tense, our impressions of being are torn by distance. That girl on the telephone should have taken a blank page and a black pencil to retrace the lines of demarcation as soon as she had put down the earpiece. But she wraps herself in the sheets. In the pillow, ensconced, the smell of the other one that she breathes while at her ear a strange voice... . Blended the voice and the smell! One and another one, perhaps joined. No retrospective psychoanalysis! The consciousness of them both has already infiltrated itself. He could not guess. She calls because of a bet, to play, she acquires a taste for it. Pleasure of the dialogue. Lying to win the friendship. She invents a story.

She tried to believe in it. She pretended. Everything was according to the norms. The rules observed. Everything weighed her down. One must believe that she did not wish for any change. She was living in this tentative situation, laughing, believing herself happy. Today everything seems so far. One must try to remember with the previous memory not to accept any interference. Four years later, she no longer was laughing. They played the game to such a degree they couldn't do without it, she pushed the

story as far as love. He was scaring the little girl still
so close to the first days in the house with the heavy
doors. She did not know the difference. Pretending
that between them, nothing was important, laughing
it off, but there was the departure which would put
kilometers between their bodies that did not know
each other yet. Why write about this minor pain? But
writing will bring the change. They have kept that
promise. For her, time had to beat to the rhythm of
Mexican letters. Imperceptibly, a new girl was opening her eyes. Michel will know nothing about it....

This departure, she wanted it, this departure
that tore her from a country she loved and from afar
she would learn to know. This departure was taking
her away from the strange voice she had not had the
time to decipher. And she was running away from an
image that she detested, she thought she had the right
to. With the severity of a little girl, she decided what
was good and what was evil. She did not admit any
contradiction. He was supposed to be perfect or he
died. The green house, the repudiated past, the child
now grown had offered all, she was taking her heart
back. This departure, she desired it without knowing
that she could not leave everything behind. The plane
had not taken her away, she will find this out later.
The lessons were also at the end of the trip.

Julia, she was now facing her, Julia, her mother, distrust and wait, the wish perhaps to be mothered, and the fear of being suffocated. New faces. A new house. A house? The green house was taking in her memory the looks of a château. In the new world, sandwich-men, sardine-families, the apartment on the fourth floor. She is learning. Life in a group.... She is learning. The loneliness in the midst of an anonymous and indifferent crowd. She understands. Her consciousness was taking in the differences and the numerous similarities. They speak of solidarity. She hears. And the reunions! Those she distinguishes in the middle of the crowd. She starts over.

TWO

I just finished setting up my bookshelves in the back room. I always leave the books for last, for the pleasure of picking them up one by one, reading the titles again, sorting them out, rearranging them, spending time connected to someone else's words.

Why this feeling? I do not know, but I feel the change will mark me. The body? The mind? The hand which draws those lines. I had not foreseen the escalation or at least not so quickly, and I have the sensation of having been pushed along not by them but by my own eagerness.

After the long months of attraction-rejection, this trip to Mexico together, without promises or compromises, has helped draw the background of our story. Upon my return, our eyes filled with laughter, I noticed that he was bringing his dirty clothes with him to wash them at my place. Quietly, without asking me for anything, he washed, dried, ironed, folded and put his piles of clothes in a little suitcase. Sometimes, without meaning to, he forgot a shirt or shoes in my drawers. After playing for a while at pretending, because love was seeping in, because I could see the troubled days elapse, I unintentionally forgot to ask him for a key lent one stormy night. We did not live together. Eli was my guest, a visitor who would call before coming over. At times, I would answer no, without a reason. Sometimes, I wanted to be alone, other times, I really had someone over. Often, Eli would show up with the tribe, and I would recapture the ambience of the street of L'Ours Blanc. It is because of them, with them, because they were there on that Christmas night, that I had to leave my apartment. Nonsense, says Eli! Don't think about it any more! Yet, he has told me often enough, he is used to it; but for me it was a shock! The discovery in my body of a difference known in theory. How have I been able to live in this country for so long without feeling a certain rejection? Eli says it is my inadequate education; the seclusion has had negative effects. Even over there, Lili, you did not learn. You are wrong! Paul always said to his little girls, looking at pictures from the four corners of the globe, that there is no difference. For the choice of friends, the color more or less brown, black or green of their skin, did not matter, nor the number of dresses, new suits or gold earrings. He only rejected the sons and daughters of bogeymen, the generic name of all those who were not on our side of the fence, and even then, the little girl protested in the name of justice. I have learned, Eli, that there could not be any difference. But you criticize the non-learning of this difference that shows in the eyes of the others. But what did we care about the others?

In this new country, the years of seclusion gone, I had still not learned; even when I started working for the Jesuits, perhaps the doctrine protected me, I did not feel anything. I was, obviously the other one, but without the *stiffness, without the empty comments, without the embarrassed stares. In the countryside, where I earned my money for my third year of college, I was the pretty foreigner. All foreigners are pretty! This point alone got on my nerves. The boys' eyes shone, the girls' eyes teased, and the children's tenderness, their voices asking why your hair, why your skin, why your words? And the adults would laugh with me, at these unchecked but not hostile words. Louise was amused by the fame that came with my status of foreigner.*

    In the streets of Montreal, I saw myself different in every shop window but did not hear cruel comments, Eli, did not perceive hostile body language. I remember registration day. These were the early days, the first days of university! Facing the secretary, I interpreted the question as a lesson, a training in modesty, not as a mark of difference. She had asked "Paul Michel, what is the first name?" I answered like a polite little girl, "It is Paul," without detecting any rejection, all the while thinking deep down "my girl in your country, your name is well-known, the name of your father, of the father of your father, your mother, the daughter of so and so, who married Paul Michel. There is no hesitation, you are Miss Michel in spite of the strangeness of your masculine first name. Here, Paul Michel, father or daughter, unknown! Put aside the certitudes of your little life, your prerogatives are relative, geographically limited; forget about the habit of being somebody because you have a father, a grandfather, a great-grandfather, at times a mother, etc., your last name is Michel, first name Paul, your file number is X, no more, no less." I did not want to see any particular sign. I had not learned, you said. That Christmas night, I learned and still this was nothing compared to the pains that some, you too, have lived in their flesh, in their messed-up bodies and even that is nothing compared to... and there's no end to it. That night, in my little apartment, racism arrived at my door like a parcel bomb. They have turned down the lever, no more electricity, no more heat, no more cooking. We had no clue, we could not have imagined the significant and deliberate gesture: the tenants alone had the key to the meter room. When I went out to check whether the breakdown was confined to the building or the neighborhood, I saw the stuffed toy, on my doorstep, a dog, and we still did not get it. I knocked at the door of the old lady whose apartment was still lit. While I was explaining the breakdown, the surprise, she listened to me quietly with a sad look. I remember your words when we went back into the apartment: "Your neighbor is crazy!" because she had shaken her head, caressed my cheek while whispering, "They are mean, you know, but above all, stupid and ignorant." We did not know who "they" were. One hour later, inside, forced to put on jackets and coats, we were discussing our departure for rue de L'Ours Blanc, when we heard a knock at the door: it was the old lady "Check the lever!" She wished us a Merry Christmas, and left. I was never to see her again. The next day, the whole tribe packed my bags and the same day I settled in the huge apartment.

They knew I need a place of my own and, for me, they made an exception: I alone will have a room, just for me, that Eli will share when I wish. It is difficult to think about what is to come.

Even if this change is just temporary, living together is already influencing the text. The tribe always respects my moments of isolation but sometimes a hand pushes the door open, a head appears and an affectionate voice asks if I am working. Yes, I am working! The word amuses me, but the definition in the dictionary forces me to think about it, "the trouble one takes to accomplish something: the labor of the mind wears men out more than physical labor." I am not taking great pains, I do not even know if I am accomplishing something! And why this distinction? I use my hands, my body, not just my head of a crazy girl! I work and they do impede my writing, less than I was afraid of, less at least than at the time of my escapes among them. There is Eli who often sleeps next to me, who wakes up and looks at me for a long time when I am seated at the table that he himself made. I write for hours. Eli says nothing, does not ask any questions, his look, at times, calms me, at other times pushes me to control my pain. His presence and his words between us have already changed the text.

We played, for many months, at pretending not to take ourselves seriously, joking about our desire to be together; we had spent the previous winter meeting by accident and seeing each other with a surprise that was never faked. Upon my return from San Francisco at the glass entrance at Dorval, looking at him waiting for me, worried, smiling in spite of the doubt, I had understood I would have to talk. This trip together, these weeks of vacation when he had offered me his tenderness, without expecting mine, my return alone, after him, for the joy of seeing him through the glass doors, this earlier trip to Mexico (my exorcism, he knew, was necessary) had to precede the first whisperings.

In spite of the words and our conversation that autumn night, he will again say, "You never want to talk." That night in the apartment with the mauve carpets, I had talked a lot; as for the rest, patience, time will be needed; as for the rest, I have already been able to tell him about the hold of the text. All lights out, in the security of a large bed, I have explained the anxiety, the wonder, and the incertitude. Now he knows. He looks at me writing, and during the hours of very high voltage, he uses the teasing tone of the earlier days: in abscissa, Paul, what's that? In those days, he did not know it all yet.

Steve

The arrival. Toward the end of a fall, I discovered this city where I was going to bury myself for so long. I love this season which is not summer that I know so well and which is often scorching, nor winter that I will never be able to tolerate. It was a hot fall, October 1970 in Montreal. You can't remember! The army in the streets, the students' unrest, the anguish of those people not familiar with the smell of violence in everyday life. As for me, I stayed impassive. My composure surprised them; they could not guess the familiar resonance of this unusual autumn; they could not know that a few months earlier, when this boat in the harbor of Port-au-Prince tried to bomb the vital areas of the city, shells had exploded on our street, damaging the window of the large room. They thought I was detached when I showed neither horrified surprise nor nausea at the tales of police bludgeoning, of interrogations, of incantations, of telephone-directory-thick-on-the-head-to-avoid-the-recourse -to-justice-from-the-victims-because-of-the-evidence-of -blows, of the police illegal activities. Illegal! In a country where policemen must respect the law, they were stunned by my silence, watching me closely for a reaction of panic, their reaction, at the sight of those military trucks crisscrossing the city. As for me, I calmly walked up and down the streets already cool, solely concerned by the ever-insufficient thickness of my coat. I understood later. Not the anger at the unjust arrests, or the astonishment at the arbitrary police controls, but the insolence, the confidence, the easy retort head upright that those policemen deserved who must respect my rights, respect the law.

With the return of silence, I started to take the first attempts at a hidden life, replicating without meaning to, the old seclusion: the apartment, the tender family, the courses, the work, the research and the wait for the summer in New York.

I told you about him pell-mell, zigzagging through memories still burning, scars still sensitive, making it difficult to lay myself bare. I have shown you the summer photos at the Mountain, where, in broad daylight, I found a place in a huge bed. It was not the first summer! I needed time and guidance because I could not, the first summer, decode the mental block. The first meeting was not in New York, he had come to be with me in Montreal. I had broken the secrecy, recovered the taste to laugh, and a year of written words had made Patricia's head explode. Her body still said no. I did not know the reasons, I did not know yet that my crazy girl's head was rejecting the unknown, disquieting bond, in my body still bristling. Our dialogue had to begin anew; these letters bringing me the pieces of the puzzle were needed: we had sworn not to cheat, he wrote to me about these amazing girls who delighted his mind and his body. I was not jealous. Not yet, I thought. I learned to be jealous in the warmth of a sleeping body. I have not talked to you about Steve, for it is said that a woman never forgets her first lover and I refused to be like the others. Steve was not my first lover, I haven't had a first lover; Steve was my answer.

We had met each other by accident inside a movie theater. My eyes must have often caught a glimpse of him in the corner where the fans waited for the beginning of the second showing because on the day I spoke to him, his face was already familiar to me. We were there almost every night and this delirious passion for the moving images amused us, made us close. He and I liked the same books, he also had the passion to write. I learned all this in between two movies that we consumed at the Cinéma Outremont. A few months later, we found ourselves together in the same course on literary creation! I did not plan anything, I was not attracted to him, I only liked spending long moments in his company discussing ideas which interested us both, especially this obsession of ours of putting down on paper our hallucinations. We would meet anywhere: at the movies, at the cafeteria of the university, at the entrance of the library, in his home, in order to talk. One evening he talked to me about the importance of desire. Shirley. I have talked about waiting for summer. Michel. I also said something else. I remember the words, these are the words that I will never forget: "I want to make love with you, and you, you would do a good deed; I wanted to choose my first lover without reasons, at random, and it is you!" He did not show the reaction of the offended male. He understood. We went to eat a hamburger, to help me be brave and later he made me listen to the beating of my heart. Because of Steve and of the happiness of the nights we will spend together, those nights when I looked at him sleeping, a stranger and yet so close, I discovered then that I would never be jealous. I keep only the words and those nights when he was not yet dreaming of locking me up.

At the Mountain, when I told Michel about the coming of pleasure, he too seemed to understand. But at the Mountain, I mostly talked to him about other things: the first reckless actions, the visit of this black woman who according to Steve looked like me, the student reunions, and the beginning of the end of my seclusion. It was really the promised summer, this summer in New York, even if it was our second summer together. It was the summer of my first steps going inward.

Montreal, December 29, 197...

Liza,

Although I sent you a letter two days ago, I am writing to you tonight. It is the letter-reflection of the month! These last days, I have been so rushed that I have not taken the time to think. There was, of course, the excitement of the Christmas season because even an outsider to this kind of celebration suffers from the repercussions of the overexcited ambiance.

I am relieved that it is over. I was fed up of being assaulted by these Santa Clauses and their debonair looks, pretending to be interested in the children when only the wallets of their parents count for them. I do not know if the mad consumption has taken hold of Christmas in my country, and if I will have to face this assault upon my return, but here this time of the year depresses me. On the other hand, I am very happy to be on vacation, to have the time to meet people that the pace of life prevents me from seeing as often as I would wish.

I ended up having a permanent position, still in the same office, where I was temping. For almost a year, I had the impression of constantly starting over, continually learning new things knowing that it would only be for two or three months! It is over. I

157

have a job. The ambiance of the new office is pleasant but I confess that my adaptation is not completely done. The university environment, even if I criticized it often, was reassuring because of its constant change, its diversity. That may seem contradictory to you, but the working world seems to me a standardizing, norm-reducing, grinding machine; besides, this is why in spite of my ferocious wish to experience real life, I am determined to secure a place for myself elsewhere. I feel the gap during my encounters which occur less and less often with those of my friends who are still students. They have kept the same lifestyle, fascinated by subjects which now leave me cold, we have fewer and fewer interests in common. I continue to see Steve, fairly regularly, a little because he too has left the university but also a little from weakness. Although we have been friends for a long time, in spite of our fling, I recently get the impression that he wishes to invent a love story. But I refuse to give in to feelings of tenderness for his favor to me. I maintain my distance! Moreover, he dreams too much of locking me up in a cabin deep in the woods and making me a dozen little Steves! Don't worry, my agenda does not correspond at all with that one....

I am stopping now, I am beginning to get hungry, and in spite of my best resolutions, once more, I am going to have a bag of nuts and a glass of milk.

I will survive!...

Love,
Paul

It is nine o'clock and I am not at the office. The apartment is quiet for a few more minutes; those who had to leave are no longer here, the others are sleeping. I am as if alone and in spite of the danger, I am not afraid. I know that soon one of them, noticing my coat near the entrance door, will come in to inquire. What's going on? Why haven't you left? I went out as usual, at the same time. Eli kissed me at the street corner and went on his way. My bus goes by very close to the building. I don't have to walk far. I stayed alone at the stop for a short while, then people arrived while I heard in the distance the noise of the bus. I remember turning back to try and make out the number; several bus lines stop there, then the sensation of blacking out. Since I was leaning against the iron pole of the bus stop I let myself slide down along the rod until I sat down in the snow and I heard the noise getting closer. And then, nothing. When I opened my eyes, I was alone. Where had the people gone who were waiting next to me? Where had the bus full of people gone, with the driver who sees everything from his raised seat? I was alone in the cold, sitting on a sidewalk in the muddy snow left by the coming spring. No matter how often Eli repeats himself, until our discussion gets stormy, until I get all on edge, until I get angry unnecessarily, I am not able to stay impassive in front of this indifference, this fear, for there are no other words for it. They are afraid and they no longer see. I know it is perhaps risky to move someone who is hurt, sick when one is not a doctor; there is also the possibility of a lawsuit. This is the cruel game of that society! I try not to judge, however; without touching or moving, it does not cost anything to call an ambulance, a doctor, anything, just a little bit of one's time. For a sick dog, some of them would have reacted. Why this criminal indifference? They probably thought I was a drug addict gone on her trip and their morals were comforted! Therefore the drug addict does not need help? Don't talk to me about the visible difference, I will not believe you; I refuse this time to hear that only the foreigner was denied their attention. How many times haven't we shuddered upon reading or hearing that a sick old woman had died because there had not been a neighbor, however informed of the situation, to call a doctor or try to come to her rescue? That the young woman attacked in the metro or in the yard of her building had stayed lying there, bleeding for precious hours when it was still possible to save her? Because the fear natural at the time of the aggression had left its imprint in the eyes of the passers-by. I want to understand the fear of the one who changes sidewalks and does not come to the rescue of the woman screaming for help, the fear of seeing the weapon turned against him explains his action. To understand but not accept. What keeps someone from calling for help, seeking help? She died alone. Why is it so often she? I discover anguish in the crowd, in the big

*city, in this society; I discover my anguish of the outside.
I had discussed it with Liza, and she, the westerner, the
city-dweller, told me she did not understand this behavior of wild beasts. Do you believe that wild beasts act
that way? I doubt it, this expression, in the end, is only a
human interpretation. Nothing is comparable to the cruelty of our species, and the humanoids who classify themselves in the so-called civilized category are even more so.*

*Alone, sitting on this frozen sidewalk, I got
scared.*

Claudine

This last study year had not held any surprise either; my reflexes of a studious little girl had worked marvelously well. I loved this work, I was thrilled by the wide range of the research and the ideas. But for me, it was the last year, in spite of my arguments with Steve, in spite of the advice of some professors who wished to see me continue, I wanted to live! I was barely making out what real life is about through my student fog when I met Claudine, the first compatriot I met whose acquaintance I had not made back home. We talked about topics I had only touched indirectly, for Claudine was already working. And we talked about the sitting men. In those days, I saw them standing, erect in a heroic quest that I dreamt of sharing. Claudine would listen, moved and irritated, recognizing in me the bursts and incurable hope of her own illusions, desiring, however to warn me, to save me from the recklessness that motivated her anger. I did not pay any attention, wanting to drag my friend along in order to give her back a sense of wonder, but she stayed on the sidelines and kept an eye over my first moves. If my recklessness did not cause irreparable damage, it is because Claudine was watching over me. I felt my way groping through a multitude of clans, trying to understand why, although all of them claimed to be moved by the same will, although all of them wanted the same results, they tore at one another so, each using up precious energy to prove the errors of the others. Claudine and Gérard criticized the manner of their methods, their inconsistencies, while I attempted to defend their profound motivations.

Facing my rage and my requests for explanations, Gérard would agree to tell the story. Later, we would make ourselves comfortable under the dining-room windows to work. I was still the student. He and Claudine explained philosophy and economy, wanting me to understand the different phases of history, the big ones, before trying to identify the little ones. I listened carefully and the presentation over, I rejected the theory. Useless, all this knowledge! I was not about to become, once more, a prisoner of books! I would much rather go toward life, real life; if I want to abandon the world of books, it's to be on the move! Gérard smiled. I would leave then, for weeks, going from demonstrations to evenings of solidarity, from gatherings to conferences, then I would return to the fold, to find again the lucidity of Claudine and Gérard's accounts. Drunk, all upset by the quarrels, hurt at times by the reactions of those for whom a woman is an equal partner for daytime discussions but who, come night time, must turn into a silent odalisk. I would find myself breathless at times. Claudine tried to curb my rage, "Don't confuse things!" They did not understand the true sense of your words! Claudine then defended while I would use feminist arguments. She would become more brutal, accusing me of putting all men in the same basket, of wanting to irreversibly trap myself, a condition for which my history did not prepare me. Already, at that time, Claudine would make me face myself: "Lili, you constantly say that you want to learn as much as possible so that upon your return home you can resist, refuse the traditions which do not suit you; but do you think that this dogmatism is positive?" She said she understood my revolt, I would say sometimes that for the men of our country, change is difficult and at other times that it was an absolute must for things to change very quickly. I got tangled up in my wishes, I wanted to go too fast. Why is real life so complicated?

Later, when I discovered and accepted that these men were in reality sitting down, squatting over, study will prevail, there were now four of us. Martine will choose to share these evenings, after the rehearsals of the group, Martine whose affinity for the theater had brought her close to Claudine and me.

The end of the year. It was for me the end of my studies, the firm resolve to stop and look for work. It was summertime! I had sent numerous job applications and was waiting. Then Michel called.

Again New York, the walks in Greenwich Village, the nights at the Albert Hotel and in the morning upon waking up I dashed to the restaurant. I am always very hungry, early in the morning, and this hotel used as a brothel did not care about the stomachs of its patrons. All day long, as during those nights, there was Michel and the uninterrupted dialogue. I would tell him all running out of breath, he was already laconic. I understood then the gray areas of the previous summers when we dreamt about life: Michel explained the limits of sharing, a part of his life that belongs only to him, friends that I will never meet. I tried in vain to imagine what were those realities, what it was that those people concealed, who those people who were forbidden to me. When summer came, I knew. I had my own secrets. I would have liked to share with Michel the discoveries, the hesitation, the evenings with Claudine and Gérard but he did not want to share. I had to make the experience alone. I would always be alone. Then, confronted with his desire for silence, I chose the generalizations, started discussing my new studies; his reactions would vary: amused, condescending, listening to my dreams and my anger, he would personify refusal, rejection at discovering my newly acquired lucidity. I was afraid, some nights at the Albert Hotel, refusing this break in my life, and, for the first time in the heat of a summer in New York, I left Michel, running away for a day or two to see other faces, to forget my demands, this yearning to share with him the shadows and the light. Michel tried to keep me away from real life, I was the little girl with the fragile neck, afraid to discover someone else, strong and determined. He let me take the first steps by myself, to make the mistakes. I will be alone to discover hell.

Another move! I feel that with Eli my story will be punctuated with boxes to fill and new furniture to build. We had decided to carry the minimum to the local district and I had sold these belongings bought with my salary (the fruit of my labor!), attaching no value to their material presence; the most important was to have a place of my own anywhere, with just about anything to live, and the tribe had understood that it was my only concern.

But here we are again, for the second time in a few months dragging along books and clothes. I don't know why we had made that decision, nor who had spoken first about looking for an apartment away from the others, in another building and if possible in another neighborhood. I only know that we are not running away from them, we are dreaming of a place where there would be one more room, one more than we needed, for them to come, for them to have a corner in our home, to tell them that any one of them has a place in our home. But the tendency is to break up, the tribe is disintegrating. In addition to ours, there is an apartment Avenue des Pins, and another one Rue St. Catherine. We laughed at the proximity of the two apartments (we on the far east side) but anyway there are two apartments, the tribe physically no longer exists. I am not sad. We must have all felt this need to be apart, to create a physical distance between us. Are the problems going to be the same? With Eli, a tentative prediction, long discussions about this new reality of our life together. Both of us admit it, there exists something else already; not something more! I reject any idea of a superior stage, of a higher level reached within our marginality, consequently the importance of not changing. I do not want any difference between my mauve apartment, my hiding place with them, and this home of ours; only the pleasure to be together in the same place, in the same bed, in the same kitchen, preparing meals together. I have always been reticent at the very idea of a life in common with someone and I maintain a critical mind to avoid being bogged down, anticipating the suffocation. I have always been afraid of it and I had good reasons to be.

Romain

It was wintertime. I remember the season because of the bar on rue St. Catherine where we met for the first time and this turtleneck sweater that I had offered him for Christmas. I had no difficulty in telling you about Michel or Steve (I could have demanded that you hear about Claudine). They stayed in me in spite of the distance, they are a part of me in spite of time. This gap between my men and me is about their transformation, a transformation which no longer suited me. I keep the men I have known, the men I have loved well or not well; but I reject some of them because of the resentment which clings to their memory. Romain had wanted to lock me up and it took me some time to become aware of it. Claudine worried about my apparent impassiveness when I tried to explain to her the importance of being sure, of not being wrong, because I wanted to give myself all the chances. Everything came at once and I feared getting confused: I had just found work a little while after meeting him and I ran the risk of making him bear the stress of my professional adaptation. Moreover, Michel still stuck to my skin. It was not easy to untangle the reasons!

This work was becoming more and more important to me as the weeks went by; it got me out of my isolation for, even after the first contact, the university world into which I had thrown myself remained a closed world, another ghetto. With this work, I entered the reality of my dreams as I told Claudine and Gérard. Romain did not want to follow. Our first fights, first difficulties to have a dialogue, our first misunderstandings, were about my relationship with work: I no longer entirely belonged to him and he was resentful of that fact, refusing to hear that I would not be, would never have been, his, or anyone else's. He called it exploitation, you are letting yourself be used. I thought don't try to enslave me, I am not yours! I thought so but said nothing, madly in love for the first time, not having yet learned to clearly delineate the limits of my territory. I wanted to love him and be myself, without yet understanding that I needed to be myself first. I was barely beginning to write the word autonomy and I thought that he knew how to read. He demanded autonomy but only for himself, when he wished and as he wished. These evenings at the club! He would make sure that his little girl was sensibly at home before going out to meet his friends. I refused to be his little girl, once again somebody's little girl and I rejected the suffocation. Should I have been suspicious? But no, not that! No matter the falls, I have learned to get up. My affection is long- lasting and my hope indestructible, and once I come out of my dreams, I still have a few intuitions. Claudine did not understand why I refused to marry

Romain as he wanted to, demanded it, even though I was powerless to end our shaky relationship. Cruel, she claimed that it would have been better to spend one week with him than these long months talking like deaf people. I was desperately trying to get him out of his shell, to make him discover the exceptional being that I knew existed inside. Arrogance, said Claudine! Tradition, the weight of thousands of years of socialization, I came to find out later. One week with him!... I could have perhaps avoided those heart-rending, wandering days.

I am walking alone in an alley. It is ten o'clock. It is summertime, the sun is just setting. I walk slowly, not being in a hurry, no one is waiting for me. Besides, no one ever waits for me, nowhere. I detest making people wait. I love walking in one direction, knowing how to follow my steps, finding the time to dream in the middle of people who live, hustle, rush around me. I am thinking about something in particular or about someone. I am smiling to myself, and a branch that sways near my face brings me back to this city, to this street. All of a sudden, a blank. I no longer know who I am, where I am, nor who are all these strangers around me. The images in my head, gone, lost, dispersed by a flash of lightning, a word or a smell. Suddenly, I am afraid to be lost in this city that I no longer recognize, lost without a face and without a name, with just a word in my head that I would endlessly repeat to those who would worry about my presence in this street: "Shiver!" Why this word? Why me, standing, mindless at the corner of Tenth Avenue, shivering, barely able to move forward because I am frozen? In the middle of the month of July, this flash of lightning that reduces me to less than nothing makes me feel cold. "Shiver!" and I recall the icy wind, the swirling snow of the Québécois winters, the skeletal trees, the hurried passersby wrapped up and anonymous, a winter that I dread for its cold, its wind, the need to be covered-up, weighted down with clothes too heavy which mask the identity of a silhouette. He often said: yesterday at noon I saw you at the corner of rue St. Catherine and St. Denis. I recognized your blue coat. They all wear the same coats, these uniform winter figures: wool or fabric, red or blue coats made by the same big chains, bought in the same big department stores....

I got the address from Lucie. I went in, it was a Thursday night. An entire row of coats of the same cut hideously identical, I asked to see something else. The saleswoman pointed at the stairs, the floor of clothes on sale, clothes which are no longer fashionable, and in the batch, the coat: awful, of a marvelous bad taste, a tight-fitting cut. This year, they are all wearing flowing coats or cloaks. The fabric resembles cheap tapestry, blue flowers on a pink-salmon background with a pale blue fur lining. It cost one hundred dollars. I insisted on a reduction: "It is too ugly, I will not pay that price!" The owner was laughing, he too knew. I got it for twenty-five dollars. Never again would he say, I saw you yesterday at noontime at the corner of St. Denis and St. Catherine! Never again did I allow him to spy on my silhouette at the corner of a street. It was wintertime during my break with Romain, winter had entered my life. And it is because of him that the last summer was to come.

To reject the fear lurking in the back of my head, the panic which was slowly eating away at me. You had crossed my life for the past few months.... A text that I had in my head like a tune one hums when waking up... Fall of 1976, fall of 76, the long walks in a gloomy Montreal under the rain! The wait! I am waiting, I had spent long months without writing, living in slow motion, swept over by this need to save others from themselves. And summer! Michel returns from the East Coast! Michel who tells me about Liza, very little about Liza: the names of the cities, the daily worries, a beautiful photo and a voice heard during their stay in Dallas. I learned nothing about her, that night at the Albert Hotel. He learned everything about those six months of torpor. He understood at the sound of my voice, that I was barely waking up, slowly coming out of my night, devastated, zombified, and I open my arms to him. He said, "You have grown older!" It was perhaps true, I knew that I was different, I had for the first time known the instinct of preservation, I had said no.

While going automatically through the motions in front of the ticket-window of the bus terminal, catching Romain's gaze, I felt my numbness ebbing away and maybe in my head, the first words of the text. At Port Authority, a few seconds, a smile and we hugged like old friends. Tens of letters, a hundred even, destroyed as we had decided, our interminable conversations, barely a few days together, and I had become his friend. One day, running out of arguments, we might have found trust, for that we would have needed practice and time. Of the two of us together, I recall only the time of the travels. I do not remember Montreal, I do not like it, besides, I do not like any city. Some cities have left no impressions on me, they have barely touched me. Foreign and gray cities. Sill, New York stays in my body, like the pale and fine scar of an expert surgeon: New York and its summer heat, New York and its ugliness, its hideous skyscrapers, its dirty streets, its ill-smelling subway, and the swarming in the obscurity of the room in the Albert Hotel. An insignificant hotel room with its cracked walls, the dubious sheets of the bed with the creaking base, the orange bedcover, last vestige of a past that it amused me to invent. I invented, that night at the Albert Hotel! Different stories. Four years. Mexico that I imagined by these pages read at a two-week interval. Did we talk about a trip to Mexico? I have forgotten. These studies that he detested. He told me everything: the cities, the classmates, the university, the discoveries, and I invented in my head our Mexican story. Paris! I deleted a complete book of his change of addresses. Letters to no end! When I destroyed those letters, they filled many bags. The same day, I tore all my notebooks: useless journal, I keep everything in my drawers. Before leaving for Montreal, I had offered him the first part, my carefree attitude, my screams of muffled rage, clearing everything out. I have not kept a journal since. My memory was these letters that he read kilometers away. Then, there was the book that I had loved bringing into the world as if it came from me. And discomfort settles in. This fictitious bond made me heartsick, this atrocious distance between us: I think that I never came to hate so much the distance than at the time of the book, and faced with the impasse, I started to run away. I cannot find the words or the empty sentences that I may have written him after receiving the book, but everything must have happened that way. I was already running away, I could not explain it to him. My only secret! To be near him, to tell him what I really thought was impossible, therefore I kept everything in. He never knew. That was the reason of my sadness the last night at the Albert Hotel, the reason of this letter telling him of my story with Romain. He wrote, I remember, that it was the letter of an unfaithful wife to her husband. This was the letter that could not tell my silence about the book: I had been unfaithful the only way I could be: I had hidden my thoughts to my friend. I did not have the courage to put everything down on paper, knowing the two-week interval, the possibility of a postal negligence (may he never receive that letter... to be forced to write it over...), his presence would have been necessary. But at that moment, the uneasiness was the strongest feeling. I did not say anything that night, nor later, I had only come to exorcise my demons already weakened. At my return, I was alone in Montreal, alone in the wet streets at the beginning of fall, in my head the first sentences of the text. I had kept Michel's book inside of me, what I could perceive, and which without knowing why was going to guide the hand of the one who writes.

Montreal, July 7, 197...

Liza,

Here I am again after a long silence. I know that you must have understood that I had to be in bad shape for not writing to you, that my silence did not mean indifference. I needed time to pause, to clarify the situation. I needed to examine, raise questions about my relationships with my circle after a new shock: I was fooled once again! You often tell me that I am too trusting, that I do not observe people well enough before throwing myself into a new friendship. You may be right but if I try to correct myself, I refuse also to distrust a priori. I do not give a damn about the difficulties.

Why should women always be the ones who give without getting back anything in return? Only tradition forces them to and I reject this kind of tradition. After six months of patience I hit back.

I have succeeded in establishing with Julia a harmonious relationship: after a time of observation, like a fighter at the beginning of a match, I took the first step from the mother which led me to the friend. My sisters are still at an age when I am forced to set the example and, in spite of a certain irritation, I bear the responsibility, understanding that this means to be both loved and detested. Obviously that includes our fights and it is better that way. With my friends, my pals, it is simpler because I have chosen them: our affinities enrich our relationships. And there it was, a man wanted to turn everything upside down. He should have been a friend, but he turned down the friendship because we did not hit it off at all, which gave him a somewhat special place. I tried to be his friend, taking an interest in what he was doing, what enthused him, what he said, and that attitude seemed natural. No reciprocity! Interminable, often stormy discussions were necessary to make him understand that I had no intention to drop those friends of mine he didn't like, nor to see his friends when I had nothing in common with them. I had to fight to do things that did not excite him, while he found it perfectly normal to pursue his activities without me. Do you know that several times he got angry at me because I would not drop the theater troupe! He judged it a waste of time. An amateur theater troupe, it does not look serious! The day of our first performance, confronted with the congratulations, he managed to make me angry: if all those people found our performance interesting, the text valid, the play of the actors not too bad, it was to flatter me and make me look ridiculous (and of course, for women this is the case!)or then to sleep with me (you are guessing with whom!). He even pushed the cynicism as far as setting himself up as an example: if he had come to attend one of our work rehearsals, it was because he liked me, that it was the best way to court me!!!

This was the last straw! I was fed up with him and sent him packing. All that has not been easy, he refused to understand, could not accept it and would not stop asking me who "he" was, because of course, it had to be because of a "he." He could not conceive that I might want to be left alone, that he was stifling me; I had to "leave him for someone else."

There you are! I have again refused to be a real woman who lets herself be beaten on and enjoys it. I feel a little bruised and I have no intention to embark any time soon in another impossible story, in any case not an affair of the heart. The little heart in question needs a vacation.

Write me soon to tell me the worst horrors, I deserve them.

Big kisses,
Paul

Alone or in the company of friends, at our place or theirs, we often talk about the return. Our conversations, whatever topic we start with, inevitably end with it. His first words openly alluded to it. He had not yet talked to me about love, he was waiting for me to decide; prudent, distrustful, he preferred the doubt to the mistake. The woman with whom he will return to the homeland! You remember! "I would like to carry you off with me, take you over there!" I had smiled at his forceful sentence: it was a question and a ploy, a question from the man caught off-guard by love, a ploy from the one who constantly had to anticipate the attack of the sitting men. It was a common practice, I did not feel offended, nor concerned by his worry. Often, to attract butterflies like him, the sitting men would use these femmes-flames who do not resemble me. I understood his mistake, I was even secretly happy at his error; so in his eyes, I was seductive enough to play the cheap Mata Hari, a trick that these phonys had masterminded. Yet, forgetting to use irony to answer the double question, I had comforted the sensitive man and the suspicious man. Without ulterior motives, I was ready to discuss with him the conditions of an eventual return to the source. The sitting men were over there, in the shadows, but they could not do anything against us, at least we hoped not!

To avoid any surprise, we had decided to talk about our stumbles: his and mine which were similar. I must tell you my revulsion. You often say that I trust people too easily, knowing perfectly well that I would not be able to contradict you for you would easily find recent examples of what you call my bad habit. Them too, I trusted them very quickly: they were using words that answered my quest. The sitting men fooled me with their beautiful, perfect sentences that unmistakably sounded like those of a sincere speech. I had known about them since the beginning, but I had no desire to join them: I was engrossed in my studies, my fear had not yet dissolved away and I felt guilty remaining deaf to the calls of the ones who knew. At the time of the first looks, I thought about them; when I sang next to this enthusiastic Italian, this lively tune in a foreign language with its words that reminded me of the sunny days in the green house; I promised myself to join the men with great courage. And I met them! Still, I did not become smarter! I understood nothing when I felt the distance between me and those who spoke in my name while denying me the right to speak. I justified it by the imperfection of the individual. I put aside my excessive demands, stifled my rage when once more I noticed the discrepancy. It was a lie, cheating! And I only reacted in front of a greater threat. I fought, I criticized, refusing to be immolated in the snow on the altar of their fame. I challenged their pretension to use me as a top model for their dishonest publicity. Then, they tried to seduce Monique! They had gone too far! They did not have the right! I showed my claws to defend someone who was still a child, not capable yet of discovering their real faces and protect herself from their duplicity.

Sitting. One will remember them sitting, if one ever remembers one day these sand statues! On the other side of the ocean, those who live at the gates of hell imagine them clad in the armor of conquerors. From the other side of the ocean, they place all of their hopes in the conquerors. Are they wrong? No one has the right to mock them, they will end up understanding. Hopefully, they do not find out too late that those who limit themselves to thunderous speeches and pronouncements do not fit to the reality around them. Here they are those fearless, blameless knights! But they do not let themselves get easily confused. To run away from them would be of no use. On the contrary, listen to them as often as possible, in order to pierce their empty words, their empty hollow ideas. Seeing them getting excited! They turn in circles in a dance that has now become macabre. To become aware day after day that they are becoming smaller and smaller, they who think of themselves as giants, for they are only worms, trying to fool their mirrors every morning. To hate these marble statues would not serve any purpose, but to scream out loud, to be certain not to take like them the habit of immobility. One will remember them sitting! In spite of their agitation, in spite of their wriggling, they are more dead than the marble statues of any muse-um. And in order not to sink, to hang on to the heritage of those still silent, within the distance, the pain deep down in one's stomach, the desire for something else. Turning one's back to any escape to which does not belong to them. She credits them with mute howls and for those screams. The screams will return. Damning!

My anger and my fear come from as far away as yours. I have lived near the sitting men, I have even caught them crouched in their uselessness. I know them, Eli, and I understand you. You feared to offend me in confiding to me your anxiety and I burst out laughing: Your tale hardly surprised me, did not even shock me, I expect anything when it is about them, even the disloyal uses of love. I was not one of them when I snuggled against you, obeying no conscious or suggested order, hav-ing never been one of their special senders. I was tough, they would not have dared. But I do not doubt for one moment that they would be capable of it.

When, even protecting your face, you were risking your security while they were accumulating capital, I was not far behind you. When I tried to resist their family pic-ture, in the effervescence of an evening, guessing their manipulation behind their smiles and their arms around my waist, you must not have been very far. We have been lucky, Eli, because, to escape from them, our fragile lucid-ity would not have been enough. For me, in addition, there was Claudine! You must have met, you too, a bruised Claudine, no longer able to think of the sun due to the indiscretion of the sitting men.

I know the importance of not hiding anything, of warning when necessary, but I fear too great a deception, the discouragement, for I am fearful of the harm they can do to us, even from afar. They must not have the pleasure of destroying us. They are not alone, Eli, there are other men besides the sitting men. We must keep our sense of wonder for the real life.

We are speaking, we are beginning to finalize our steps. I will end up understanding that this return was an integral part of our love. The long path to the source had started.

She has left again. We come back from the airport tired, tense and we choose to be silent. We will have to analyze the situation later. Marie whom for ten years I had been dreaming of with my heart of a little girl, whom I had been writing about for two years using Lili's memories, I saw her leave teary-eyed in spite of her resentment. I had waited so long for that moment when Eli would meet Marie. He had until then only shared the love of Julia and the screams of the girls. For his sake, I wanted him to retrace the way to the first day: Marie and Paul (their brief glances in New York did not count: Paul had guessed. Eli barely tried to show some interest in this man about whom I had told nothing yet.) We had wanted Marie, waiting to explain to her our choices and her first words, her first gestures had meant a rebuff: she rejected everything as a whole without listening to us, without hearing the trust in my voice. And these vacations, this meeting which was supposed to get Eli closer to my first story, were spent explaining our decisions: Marie was speaking another language! To the supplications succeeded the tears, the blackmail. And yet she had said at the beginning, that the Pope accepted etc. etc. etc. I had understood her need to be reassured, comforted. For us, it does not make any difference, when we deem it necessary, we will get married; otherwise we will live together. For us, there isn't any difference! I explained, and she had smiled in New York. She was crying in Montreal. Facing my only fit of anger, she had chosen to believe in my bad faith: I was the guilty party, I was refusing to marry Eli. Because ... and she found explanations: Paul's divorce, his negative example. I was wrong, distance had muddled everything. Marie did not accept. Autonomy, understanding, I said I was tied to this man by something else than a piece of paper, by much more than a piece of paper. She gave us her gold wedding ring and held it out to Eli. Take my ring, marry her, force her to trust you!

There could not be between us the least constraint. Marie could not understand it. How many
truths hadn't time and distance distorted in me. Eli
has never met Marie.

Martine

Autumn. I am breathing again, going out in the streets to see life once more, the people around me, and it is in that ambiance, on a rainy afternoon, with this fine and cold rain that I liked to feel on my face, that I met Martine. With her, a new friendship, a different tenderness, through her other faces go by without leaving any impression; no one could reach me besides her. I was floating in a new sensation of well-being that I wanted to keep, as long as possible, the apathy of the blissfully happy, halo and diaphanous wings.

I want to get involved in the theater: together, we make up games that make us laugh, we are mad and sad at the same time. I want to go to the movies and I discover we like the same films, that we share the same dreams, that she is my double, my positive side when I feel my wings open, my negative reflection before her impassive face and her will not to be too different. Then, I get enraged! But she continues to cross my life; I like her different stride, her smiles of incomprehension, I evaluate the risk to be taken as a model with hatred at the end, I accept the challenge because she forces me to see the world, forces me to hear the voices around me, she gets me out in Montreal white with the first snow falls. And in the mass of moving faces, that of a carefree, cheerful boy, the companion of our mad races, too different from me and from rejected images to give me a reason to be distrustful or avoid his stupid laugh. A survivor of winter-tearing crises, I had wanted isolation, brushing aside a surge of lust because my pain was still there. I wanted to be caught in a whirlwind. I was not on my guard. Martine understood before me, refusing to give him my phone number while I was not afraid. I could not be afraid of a man who laughed even when I did not want to see anyone. Later, I did not put up a fence, he made love laughing. He makes love laughing! I was coming out from several months during which simplicity had escaped me, pouring through my body and he, with distracted hands, barely touches me. Another winter begins, I will get back the tenderness, with time and patience. Another winter begins and I am healing from my long inertia. Eli, if I tell you about Martine, it's because of the misunderstanding between the two of you. You are often provoking, exaggerating your attitudes and opinions, which are but masks to hide your feelings, and Martine would flare up, would criticize your believing in the reality of these images you projected to outsiders. She told me once that she did not recognize the Eli I spoke of.... You passed each other without noticing each other even though you shared the same apartment. Martine does not confide easily, it took me time to understand her secretive nature.

(Moreover, I am not sure to have completely succeeded.) I saw in her only the friend to advise in her studies, the companion who shared with me my multiple experiences, following behind me or with me a path whose limits I had not yet marked out. During that winter, Martine fulfilled my needs, and yet, she was pulling me along; she perhaps sensed that it was urgent to put an end to my solitude, to chase away these monsters that followed me day and night, sneering at my sadness, making faces to extinguish my timid outbursts of laughter. Martine pushed me to go on particularly with my writing, guessing before me the antidote to the poison. For our troupe, it was a time of trial and error. We passed from one play to the next, trying to think of a possible performance from one of the works we loved; but very quickly we understood the difficulties of such an undertaking. *Bouki nan paradi* or *La Tragédie du Roi Christophe* were beyond our possibilities. And this was the first attempt... I placed the typed pages on Martine's lap at the moment of leaving. She called me an hour later and the next day a copy was given to every member of the troupe. Martine was interested not only in the script but especially in my offer to transform it starting with the staging and interpretation. It consisted of an outline with the ideas, the progression and the profile of the characters, a few dialogues, and my job was to consolidate the whole. When a voice exclaimed, "The character cannot say such a line!," we discussed it right away and I would end up offering another one, suggesting a tone, a movement to convey what we felt. Martine was a good listener, and at night, after our rehearsals, she would suggest to me new possibilities. When at the end of the summer, after months of work, Claudine announced to us that we had obtained a contract, in spite of our joy, we were all worried sick at the idea that we might not meet our expectations.

There was a crowd at our first performance. Yet, I am still alone.

The room is plunged in darkness, I realize that in this place there are people I know, I am happy I cannot see them when I take possession of the stage before the lighting technician makes his first move. I sit up front, as expected in the script, motionless for a few seconds, just time to wait for the lights and time to forget who I am. I feel my heart beating faster. And suddenly, another person is born. I play. This script written by me seems to me written by a stranger. I believe that, when I am the other one, it is easy to write, easy to direct a play: rehearsals, anger, enthusiasm. I would like to divide myself up and watch as an outsider the encounter of these three women, each one who believes each one of them to be the depository of the others' experiences. The play over, I hold a special fondness for the comedian, she alone had to forget the other women, the other lives, to forget herself during these minutes on stage in order to be the woman emerged on paper from our three memories. She alone had to put aside the malaise of these feverish days. When I write, life or the living sometimes interfere, imposing on me their obsessive presence. Later, explaining to the others how to say their lines or how to move about in order not to say yet say, sometimes in the middle of our work, tension mounting, I would find new distractions. This evening on stage, when the lights came on, I had to switch off in order to forget the woman I had just seen....

The Escape to Egypt. I no longer remember where I have seen this painting. In a school book? A museum in New York? A postcard sent by Paul? What importance? The Escape to Egypt. It's me, this woman with the anxious face.... Why this fear? For whom? The child? Anticipating that something will happen, predicting the future?

Did she know that this child was going to change the face of the world? This painting fascinates me, I do not try to know whether this woman had lived, whether this child is the one they pretend it is to be, the story in itself is enough because it is terrible, because it is hard to destroy, like all the stories that men accept and refuse to see die. My desire of you is a story told from generation to generation. I am afraid of your face discovered by accident in the depths of my memory. Your hand in mine! If you take the time to wait, I will tell you the power of hands, when you hear me you will know that I like your hands. The surprise in your eyes when my hand touched yours, I was burning with the desire to put my lips on your hand! I know nothing about you, only that your smile moves me, that your hands are beautiful, that your gaze makes me want to laugh. One night or one day you will find out that my most beautiful attribute is the ability to laugh, but perhaps you will never know! My naked shoulders against the leather bench, my eyes unintentionally catching yours, then you looked away. Or was it me, it does not matter, they found themselves. I no longer heard the others, I no longer saw anything, I no longer knew anything except that fear and pride were disappearing and that I no longer wanted to hide anything. I was begging with my eyes to reveal my secret to you when my lips sometimes attempted to hide it. My eyes screamed my desire for you. Did you understand? Did my eyes tell you of The Escape to Egypt? It was too late! I left.

It was necessary to forget, for the sake of the

play, and of the scriptwriter, to leave you for this character who looks a little like me. Why this distance?

We only had one male character in that play. We only had one man in our troupe, the husband of... almost an accessory, a woman made-up could have interpreted this caricature of a man. Claudine accepted this inequality in the troupe, justified by this first play, pretending to ignore that never would I want to write a text where a male actor would be indispensable, refusing my choice but avoiding the confrontation. She respected and approved my rejection of the sitting men, not my march toward women. I did not wish to force my desires on her. I wanted to show women who were mad, unhappy, tender, cheerful, cruel like those I finally had in front of me after my botched upbringing, those to whom I finally opened my arms knowing that I had finally reached the harbor. Claudine loved the theater; we had recognized each other but she refused to follow me elsewhere. Martine alone will understand that the theater was another expression of my enthusiastic march toward women, that intuition which early on had made me take sides, take action for the one they wanted to set up as my rival. And when Claudine demands a text dealing with "serious" subjects, it will be time to go our separate ways! From my experience with the theater will remain the women and a manuscript lying in the bottom of a drawer.

I love memories on glossy paper. Slices of life regained months or years later. One never deliberately catches sadness in snapshots but the smiles at times look like grimaces.

Coming back from work tonight, I felt like recapturing summer still so close and pulled out the albums from the bottom of the wardrobe. First page, first image, the first days of summer. Eli and Pierre in the foreground, Lucie and I in the background. Pierre helps Eli with his tie, and we are looking at them laughing. After the ride from Montreal to Ottawa, we had arrived, just on time at the right address. Our wedding! The word puts me on edge and the adventure still amuses me. Our wedding was to take place that day and we had wanted to turn it into a picnic with Julia, Ginou, Lucie and Pierre, only them, with us for a day in the sun. I had tried in the morning to take refuge in being provocative. Lucie had protested, Lucie had brought that English embroidery dress which made me look more like a first communicant than a solemn bride. She had said, "No jeans, Paul, don't exaggerate! The guy is capable of refusing to marry you and we would have done this trip for nothing. Don't act like an idiot, I am bringing you a brand new dress, I just bought it, it is pretty and will look well on you." I screamed on opening the package. A white dress, you are the one who is exaggerating! Why not a crown and a long white veil? Lucie did not acknowledge my anger. "If it is all the same to you, put the dress on! It does not mean anything, you know it, then why be afraid?" I was not afraid, not of the dress. But the worrisome feeling of encroaching conventions, of being stifled by the usual upbringing, was coming back to me. Had Lucie unconsciously fulfilled my expectations? Or did she want me to confront my contradictions?

Little did her reasons matter, I did not feel like listening again since I had accepted this ritual, this social constraint; the provoking jeans were only belated and childish fits of rebellion. But that day, during my moment of anger, I was suspicious of everybody: Julia and Lucie going to buy that dress together, and why not Eli with them? I wear this pretty dress in all the photos. Upon my return home, when I wanted to give her back the white dress, my friend laughed in order not to set off my anger: "You would give your wedding dress to someone?" I had already forgotten my doubts. So I have a wedding dress on glossy paper and in a wardrobe. Superstitious, every time I wear it which rarely happens it makes me look like Iphigenia waiting to be sacrificed. I feel foreign, besides, funny stories always happen to me. That dress must still retain Julia's joy on that summer day. Because, for her, it was one less "worry." Fred's death had drawn her closer to Eli; although the legal tie was missing, he was the only one that she could lean on, Eli on one side, I on the other. We held her hands to with-

*stand the hypocritical condolences, and Eli kept an eye
on the grasping vultures who were taking advantage of
her confusion to try and carry away watercolors, unfinished drawings, anything and everything that might fall
into their hands. Fred, in dying, had become a valued
commodity.*

*At night, we slept next to her and during the day,
no one dared to pretend they did not see Eli as in the past.
But Julia remembered. In spite of the tenderness, the
respect after three years, she was relieved to see that; we
had conformed to the rules of society. She obsessively
feared those men that she heard whispering, "She is the
mistress of...," and she knew that they were thinking "if
she sleeps with him, why not with me?" It was useless
explaining to her over and over again that she should not
give any importance to these rumors, that I myself did
not even hear them; she continued to be hurt by them.
When I announced that this time, that was it, in spite of
the true reason that I did not hide from her, she felt
relieved. Because there was a reason: the return which
alone justified this procedure, useless otherwise. We had
decided not to waste our energies, once back home, fighting against the stupid prejudices. In spite of Paul's reluc-
tance, which I knew for having discussed it, I had made
up my mind to eliminate any controversial subject. Was
I right? I only told Paul after the picnic in Ottawa.*

The real preparations and the real excitement of

the adventure were not tied to the "ceremony"; there was the departure. Those much-awaited vacations. With Liza. I had dreamt of Sweden, Spain, endless discussions, and England had been our choice. I was therefore set to leave for Paris, with Eli, meet Liza there to take off for the big island. Two weeks with Liza! Turning the page. The photos of Liza and me in the streets of London. We took no pictures in Paris where, overjoyed to be with Liza, I refused to see the tension between Eli and Michel. I was not paying attention to their harsh voices. I was with Liza.

Eli had said, "I will be back in Paris within ten days, call me to let me know when you are coming." I had the impression when I took the first train that those days would go by quickly. They always go by too fast. And it's over.

— What is this train waiting for?

I had the same thought at the same time as she had. I would have preferred to be alone, to have no one accompany me to the train station. In the movies, they never show these painful details: being forced to buy a special ticket in order to extend the goodbyes to the door of the couchette compartment. Even affection has a price. I feel like crying because of Liza. Why leave her at the time when I had the strongest desire to be with her, talk to her, play with her hair while Marian talks about Edinburgh? I gave you a real woman hairdo! and she laughs at our complicity above all suspicion. We will never be real women, we will only be she and I playing at being lost in the trees of Dean Village. What is this train waiting for? It leaves, I kiss her once more and I feel even more like crying. In the compartment, a lady continues to play with words I do not understand. The next day in London, I saw this stranger leave, I only exchanged a few smiles with her. Then begins the wait, long, too long! Scottish ghost stories kept me entertained but did not touch me. The train, the fatigue, the sea and the white cliffs of Dover. The white birds which fascinate me, circling in the sky, way up above the boat, and the white cliffs of Dover.

He is wearing a green shirt and jeans. He looks at the sea through the little square of his camera, then at me for a while, but I am not the sea and I do not go along with his game. Once again, he insists; I am already elsewhere, he has failed to keep my attention. I am completely absorbed by the swell of the waves which makes the boat dance. Near the Exchange booth, I hang on to the railing of the stairs, hoping for a bigger wave that would knock over all those people who come and go, as if the sea wasn't there. I feel its presence with every one of my heartbeats, all the while feeling fine, not at all afraid. I go back up to the deck to smile at the beautiful old ladies. I dare smile at all the women that I will not get to know on this boat, but who will never interpret this smile as an attempt at seduction. It's nice to be able to smile at the old ladies and the young women dancing on the deck. Ten years younger and I would have had the indulgent smiles of old men. I am too old, I am a woman, their values have changed; young and old, I am not worthy of their superficial affection. The customs officers are the only ones still capable of offering me this spontaneous gesture, unfinished and fleeting, this stealthy glance already directed at others.

And on the train, I become a decrepit Englishwoman. They are there, all three of them, they would be asked for their IDs at the entrance of a nightclub. Too bad for their solitude. Liza reserved this place. I settle in. The woman also. The two men leave with their suitcases for the next compartment. He is wearing jeans and a green safari jacket.

I am thinking about Liza and those days too short: London and its taxis, the hotel room with the loud blue bedspread where I never stopped taking her picture, the red double decker buses that we took for the pleasure of going to the very top, Big Ben where Liza announced drily that this monstrosity was once again fast, my marvelous solitude in the middle of the museum crowd, Liza's hurry and our copious breakfasts to economize on lunch. The train for Cardiff where I examine for the first time the clichés attached to the English countryside. But I am holding you back, Marie-Hélène, you made us miss the Welsh country! We were looking forward so much to our arrival at Cardiff, curious to discover the mining country. Liza hoped to find her friend or at least a note from Marie-Hélène indicating her whereabouts but found nothing, and in front of the closed door, we felt a moment of panic: our loneliness in this unknown city, the uncertainty of a possible return by Marie- Hélène forced us to walk back to the train station, the long road on foot. In spite of her absence, Marie-Hélène could not stop us from bursting into laughter in front of this dilapidated hospital and this delicious sign: "Mr. Peppercorn professor of singing, bel canto and breath control." The song of the birds while we pretended to be afraid and the train again at the end of the day. We took so many trains over these few days! If I am forgetting much, I am left with the noise of the trains and the foolish things we did to spend the time that seemed too long until Edinburgh. We feared another Marie-Hélène but Marion was there, with her passion for this city, for Scotland, and with her explanations, even when I only wanted silence. Marion and her contagious passion, the flowers and trees of Edinburgh, the color of the air at the end of the day, lilac, purple, this shade that I love and that I am absolutely unable to name, there was the joy to be with Liza. The entire country of Scotland brought back to this color: the heather on the hills that Liza shows me from the window of the train, even the green of Dean Village shows a hint of these nuances: neither lilac nor violet, both and neither.

He enters the wagon in his jeans and green shirt. He speaks to the woman who becomes animated at the sound of the familiar voice. I thought she was Italian, I did not dare to speak to her, she answers in Spanish and I smile at this language sweet to my ear. Do you understand, he says? A little, just a tiny bit. Fernando joins us, I will know his name only later, (In the restaurant of the Gare du Nord, I say to the woman "I do not even know your name." She laughs. It was true, we had not even introduced ourselves to each other. Besides, what does it matter?) Fernando has joined us, sitting on the seat in the corridor. We talk until we get to Paris: they, slowly, so the words reach my mind; I, with my hands more than with my mouth. Anyway, I play the part of the translator for the three young people. I have fun. They think I am Anglophone. Quebec, my love! These two boys with the singing accent of Provence, this girl who tells about her Chinese mother having lived in Vietnam and the curiosity of the boys in front of her different face, white-trash prejudices repeating the absurdities of several generations of racists. They coo "They are pretty, the little Chinese girls"! The "little" Chinese girl, of course, all the Chinese girls are little, all the Jews are stingy, all the blacks are lazy and all the women are whores. Except for their mothers! I am cross with them to have made them so narrow-minded. I scream at them "and the Chinese, you idiots, what are they like, the Chinese men?" Their stupor makes me burst out laughing and they think it's a joke. But they concur with each other at last: "Ah, the Arabs! We are not racist, Madame, we have nothing against the Arabs, they are just like other people. But their oil! They piss us off with their oil! Their petro-dollars! They take the liberty to scoff at us with their wealth, they are buying our houses, buying France when our government was sinking because of overspending.... Arab money smells bad, their bad taste, their arrogance and this distressing, unscrupulous ambition!" I listen to these train conversations, this bragging of little Westerners, exchanges forever frozen, and the discomfort of the "little" Chinese girl who does not dare to express her justified disgust. When the day comes, it will be too late, she will have internalized the speech. And when I think specialists lament the lack of interest of the young generation for current affairs! They are well-informed these boys!

Well-deformed! Ready to reproduce the beautiful speeches and daily racism! I shake my head sadly. They are speaking of what, he asks? I try to explain brainwash in Spanish. He does not understand, he believes they are playing. "A very candid dialogue," he says. Why candid? Because they are less than twenty years old? Why would candor belong to this age? Why candor? Candid what?

Liza would have understood, I would not have had to translate. My furrowed forehead, my clenched fists would have shown her the anger back once more. How sheltered we were during those days too short! The others did not affect us and the harmony between us avoided misunderstandings. When Liza suggested long hikes on foot, in spite of my weakness, I accompanied her; when my back and my feet started to hurt, I did not have to tell her, she would guess, and we would walk back home where, at night, deep down under the feather covers, we continued our *rêverie* whispering so as not to disturb Marion. At Inverness, both of us alone on the northern beaches that I was discovering, in front of the grey sea, constantly moving about because of the icy wind, I kept taking pictures of Liza as if deep down I feared I would be unable to go with her again to the end of the world. Somewhere in me, I already knew it, because the wedding, which had enabled me to take this vacation, was the prelude to the Return.

Gare du Nord, three Colombians a little lost keep me away again from Liza. A hotel room to find, I suggest Rue Monsieur le Prince. I must call my companion to find out. This was the moment! But he said, "If it works, I will kiss you." I call my friend, Eli: I am bringing three friendly Colombians with me, is it all right with you? Yes, of course yes, you accept, you even accept my voice soft with fatigue. I see his jeans through the glass door, I go out and he kisses me. We walk out looking for a taxi. He walks, in spite of the fatigue of the trip, the cool air of the night, this pain in his leg which resists my healing thoughts. I ask *"Como se dice?"* pointing to the sore spot, he answers and a few days later I have already forgotten. I keep only the pain, not even successful at getting him to cry, *un muchacho no llora.* If you knew how much I love the man who learns to cry! But you resist the pain, refusing even to speak about it. Anyway, let me tell you about Eli's knee. *Quien?* My friend, my companion. Second attempt! Unsuccessful. I try and I try, I order my lips to move and my memory stirs without moving. My Spanish courses are forgotten and I blame my incompetence. I will say nothing to Joaquin and it will no longer be the same pleasantness.

Eli's eyes shine in my mind. I see the reflection of his body in the window darkened by the night. He hears our dialogue perhaps. I make this boy speak in a language I barely understand, to find out about his life, his choices. *Mi Padre*! I love his love for the father staying over there. It is closely akin to my old passion, still burning, my will to break the hold through the analysis of mistakes, past, present and future. Yours also, you desperately try to justify his weaknesses! A liberal, you say, forgetting about the opposition to progress. Fine! I listen to you and I say to you that my hang-ups are different. I am hurting elsewhere. And we will be forced to kill them one day! Shut up, Joaquin, I detest psychoanalysis. I do not want to kill anyone, only to tell you about the man who took the time to become vulnerable, time the heiress needed to come to accept the possibility for errors.

I question you non-stop. You protest, and kiss me. But the impatience in me! To free your lips from too futile an occupation! You speak of the night, sleeping next to me, "Your skin is soft!" you say. I answer that I do not want any of these sentences. While Eli, on the next bed, looks at the contractions on my face that he can no longer decipher.

We will not sleep together because of the first silence, and I try to salvage the maximum. You want to lead our story toward sweetness, without understanding the misunderstanding of the train Calais-Paris. I feel like screaming. The words held back until the departure!... Why didn't you call as promised? Did you understand why my hands were so cold, the last day? I did not even kiss you to tell us good-bye....

I know, Eli that you do not accept the sudden impulses of my heart and flesh, you demand logic, self-discipline even in my fleeting affairs. When it comes to yours, you always have a sensible explanation. Me, I do not look for one and I aggravate your need for the reassuring rationalization. I say a sudden impulse of the body and you pretend to understand. Why do you repeat the same aggressive words when I whisper impulses of the heart? There are faces that have gone through me without catching on to any of my angles, while others have made their marks from my body to my heart. I know that I must explain it to you. I have at times, me too, my bit of logic, but at other times, I imagine love stories and in somebody's eyes, I discover one of those lost characters. Like every story, the dénouement can surprise; I take the risk each time because I sometimes get the character wrong. You want to get to know someone, take the time to discover tenderness, I know your words, but our story is not a universal reference. Why are you afraid of my outbursts? Their true meaning escapes me, I am even afraid of discovering what my moments of madness mask. You say the irrational, I refuse to listen to you, to know, because deep down, I too am a little afraid of my outbursts.

Liza

For many days now, I have been trying to talk about you, but the words do not come, I cannot tell, I cannot write about Liza. I don't know how to describe Liza. Why? In a moment of relaxation, I think I have found the right words, the words that would give you the key to this story, and I open my mouth, silence settles in: sentences, words, the entire construction crumbles down. If you knew what a simple story it is! Happy people do not have a story... Why do I have this sentence in my head when you want to hear about Liza. In a roundabout way, a comedian's trick?

The décor: this apartment that you will not know, my very own bedroom, a little room, where I am at home, that bears my imprints. I was, sitting on the floor, reading Michel's American letters. After the last summer in New York, we had kept the tie, a fragile bond, for no reason. Already because of Liza; without knowing it? In my little room with the unusual colors, black and white (the color mauve will come later!) I pick up the phone, this call to Michel I have no memory of, nor of the pretext, nor of the words, nor of my conversation with him, only the voice of a woman that I had never met. "Good morning. This is Liza!" Words, our meeting, going to Montreal, I, you, fast words, come! She rings at the door and at the first look, I felt that it would not be a story to erase quickly. Love at first sight for Liza! She should have been just passing through in my life, instead she stayed. The day of her arrival I made a space in my little room and we never spoke about Michel. Except our laughter when she talked about the veto. "Why do you want to meet her?" He was afraid, Liza! On the phone, the second night he expresses his worry. Tell me, he said to Liza, what happened, Michel asked me. We will tell nothing to this man who thought (hoped?) for a rivalry, jealousy, and his panic at the incomprehensible harmony. We talked, during those days and those nights, talked a lot, for we were both exploring. You were still a blur in my life, Romain was becoming a memory. Liza settled herself in without waiting. Two meetings close together in space and time! While I still had an affair with a man and no longer trusting them, for women, I did not demand any rite of passage. The words came to us and we recognized them. She looked at my books, opened them, smiled in front of an underlined passage, women's books, women's talks on mattresses placed on the floor, women's projects. I was giving birth to a lucid woman, when Liza appeared, standing in the doorway. Precious, she will witness the deliverance and eyes wide open I observed my Siamese sister live. It was the first time. She was the first woman with whom I shared many affinities. There will be others. Later. Before Liza, I alternated between the apprentice and the role model; with her from the first instant, I understood that it was possible for us.

Eli, those words appear cold to me but I have no others. Will I be able one day to describe Liza with other words? Will I be able one day to tell you? Two meetings brought closer by time. I had known Liza for some time already, you more recently, mostly you had no precise place in my life. How difficult it is! I do not succeed in really telling... I even prefer to forget my memories, invent a story. What about you telling it? If I made you tell a story to replace the words about Liza with other words, Liza's love? Close your eyes, forget who we are, nothing else exists but my voice whispering what could have been, in a place which somewhere exists, in a time that may already have been.

She wore a long multicolored checkered skirt and a plain t-shirt when I saw her for the first time. We had come to pick her up, with Martine, to drive her to one of our evenings. Always interested in a new face, in a new recruit for those weekly evenings, in spite of our feeling lazy and having started our glasses of rum, we had agreed to go and pick her up.

It was winter, she was wearing a funny wool skirt and a white cotton t-shirt, when she opened the door, then she smiled at us.

— Hello. I am ready!

And turning toward someone we could not see:

— I will be back late, don't put the chain on! I will see you tomorrow.

She took her coat and closed the door without having given us, Marco and me, a good look. She did not seem to take us for anything more than chauffeurs at her service, Martine, alone, interested her. The blank look (curious, interrogating or even indifferent, if not absent-minded) made me immediately dislike her. I found her skirt outrageous, it hugged her hips very tightly and was very wide at the bottom, her black suede boots, her sensible tee-shirt and especially her blue coat with its golden buttons.

— I had to call your office three times before getting you, reproached Martine.

She answered laughing:

— I am unionized, I am entitled to breaks.

This woman did not fit well with us. She was already working while almost all of us were still students. She lived with her parents, and we, anywhere we could. She wore a long skirt to come to one of our gatherings while, for us, the top of fashion consisted of hemming our jeans. This girl would not feel comfortable with us and I no longer felt like being next to her, but I kept on going down the stairs, looking at the fingerprints on the walls, the numbers in descending order on the apartment doors, and from time to time, the fragile neck of a skinny girl sticking out of her great blue collar.

Our first encounters will leave me with an impression of surprise often associated with her clothes. That night, I spent almost all my time with her. I made her dance even though I felt like I had been chosen from the shelves of a toy store. She would turn toward me, stretch out her hand without a word, and drag me to the middle of the room. When at her request, I brought her a drink, she would take it with a sweet, absent smile as if she did not see me. Sometimes, she would move away after putting her hand on my shoulder and I would see her, later, dance with Marc or someone else. Even with Martine, without looking provocative for it. I was not in the least shocked to see these two girls, cheek to cheek, swinging slowly. Martine seemed moved. I felt her body telling us, "She wanted to dance with me, too bad for you if you refuse to understand." She, nothing! Her body expressed nothing, her shut eyes were no different from those that I looked at when she was spinning around with Marc in the middle of the room. She just was dancing with Martine because she felt like it and it would have been ridiculous to be shocked. Sometimes she opened her eyes, catching my gaze, and would absentmindedly smile at me. After each dance, she would come back and sit next to me. Her skirt spread like a corolla on the rug. That skirt got on my nerves; the more I looked at it, the more I found the usual decoding inadequate. This outfit on another woman would send a very specific message. On her, no and yet, I clung to the sign. I wanted her to abide by the conventions, to be a flirt, a woman wanting to be seduced, but her behavior contradicted this, her easy attitude among our jeans frustrated me. She should have felt out of place. I had the impression of being the only one to notice the difference.

At dawn, Marc asked her to accompany us to our apartment, to stay with us a little longer and take the time to talk. She listened attentively to these requests and answered in a calm voice.

— Thank you, but take me home! Tomorrow, I must clean the house and I want to rest a little before then.

A sensible little girl! But would a sensible little girl have said those words?

I did not feel like seeing her again, I did not feel like seeing Martine's friend again, Martine herself seemed rather hesitant at the idea of a second meeting. She regretted having introduced this girl to us, as if we did not deserve such an honor.

The following Saturday, one hour before a cousin's wedding, I called her.

— Hi, it's Eli, Do you remember me?
— Of course, I was waiting for your call.

She said that without irony, not aware that this remark might sound surprising.

— I called your house this week meaning to talk to you, but, each time, after a long conversation with Martine, I forgot.
I thought I only wanted to hear from her in passing, and after a few minutes, I invited her to this wedding where I feared I would get bored. I was waiting for her to turn me down, to come up with an excuse of not having the time, the right dress, anything.

No reaction! I insisted:

— I have to pick you up right away, it's quite far.

— Okay, come right away. I just have time to take a shower.

— I could hear her laughing while she was hanging up.

When she opened the door, she already had her handbag, and to my great surprise, she was wearing a dark green jumper and a calico shirt. This time again, her face showed no sign, not even a hint, of make-up. I felt like telling her that we were going to a very fancy wedding, not to a picnic but I stood there, happy to see that, once more, she had succeeded in surprising me. I felt, I knew, that she had only taken a shower before putting on the first clothes that she had found in her wardrobe.

— What were you wearing when I called?

— What, why?

— Your clothes?

— I was wearing a light dress, it's hot in the apartment. Why?

— Nothing!...
I had made the effort of putting on my wool

pants and long sleeve-shirt, knowing that the relatives would still not be satisfied but it was out of question to go out of my way by wearing a jacket and tie. This girl in a jumper will be seen as a provocation, a deliberate offense on my part.

At the door of Evelyn's drawing-room, confronted by offended looks, she whispered in my ear:

— You could have warned me, she said, teasing.

— Would you have worn a long dress?

— I would have worn my Mexican necklaces and my Périclès gold earrings.

I saw her ironic smile and Martine, in the back of the room, looked at her tenderly. She moved among the groups, a real lady, smiling and talking:

— I am happy to meet you. Eli has often spoken about you.

My parents were looking at her, astonished. Later, my mother will say, "The day I met her, I understood that you were going to fall in love with her."

What amused me the most, however, was seeing her play the comedian: looking very serious, she mimicked those she had just shocked. Her imitations came from the depths of her memory: those gestures, those words, those body movements, she knew them, she had learned them in another time and one felt that they must have been part of the codes of a sensible little girl's childhood. She had certainly rejected those dull rituals that banned inopportune questioning, choosing what suited her in these customs that belonged to a certain circle. Hers! I often noticed some of her ill-timed reactions that her spontaneity made one forget or forgive. In a group younger than ours engrossed in a dispute, she would caricature, adopting this style they were spewing out, more *bourgeoise* than the worst of them. We could not hold it against her. The following day, she was our image, enlarged, our critical reflection. And she would laugh at our rebellion. The only people she respected were those who still knew nothing about rebellion. I understood it the day when her eyes got somber.

I had been seeing her for some time already. I knew about her what she allowed (sometimes, rarely) to let out. That time, I had not been able to guess whether she was kidding. She had called me very late.

— Eli, you are sleeping? Shake yourself a bit. I need you.

I like the way she ignored my own wishes; She needed me, needed me to drive her out of town, and after ten days of silence, she was calling me.

— You were supposed to call me last Saturday.

— Eli, it's urgent. We will fight later. Can you come and get me?

— I am coming.

— Dress up appropriately!

I did not know the reason for this rush. I did not know what to make of her advice, asking myself if it was a new game. In the car, she looked at me without saying anything. She had only given me the address, on a street on the eastern side and seemed to be lost in thoughts, forgetting my presence. In front of the building, she asked me to wait.

— I am coming with you, this neighborhood is not safe!

— I told you to be suitably dressed. You can't come in like that.

— What are you talking about? In this neighborhood, people are dressed that way! ...

— They have to, Eli, they would not appreciate your mimicking.

In her voice, no reproach.... It was four o'clock in the morning when she came out, haggard, red-eyed, exhausted because of someone or something that I did not know about.

— Let us go to your house. I don't feel like going home.

In the apartment, she still kept quiet. Then, having drunk a glass of milk, she went to bed, without explaining. I had decided not to ask her any questions. The next morning, she told me that she had turned twenty-six years old the day before.

She was the one, a few days later, who reminded me of that evening. She was trying to talk to me about the young woman who wanted to die, the child she was expecting, the other three kids to bring up, the irresponsible man who had just left them. I did not understand her connection with the pregnant woman, but she was not listening to my questions, she wanted me to understand without explanations, and I remembered only her red eyes, her face aged by a drama that should have never affected her. That day, she had opened a little door, I was fighting to keep my foot in the corner. She had to speak! I was asking her questions and, seeing her getting upset, I felt the moment was not far when she was going to scream the essential words. Seated on the floor, I was caressing her ankles, she was ensconced in a wobbly armchair. She had closed her eyes at my insistence. In the next room, Martine was getting the meal ready. I was afraid she might call me, that it was my turn, my day to cook, but the silence of the room where we were must have been so heavy that Martine did not dare to intervene.

When she began to speak, it was with such a soft voice that I could not catch the sense of her whispered words. I was listening for the first time. I will often reproach her for her silence, she will always answer, "I don't know how to tell!" That evening, she talked about pain and blood, rage and powerlessness in the face of those centuries of training, and I could not really share her knowledge. I was hearing sentences that scared me. Why was this girl that I thought carefree, cheerful, that I wanted to be irresponsible, superficial, trying to lead me into a world too dangerous for my security? I did not want to understand when she told me about the life of a woman and, perceiving my fear, she guessed that I was trying to resist the proffered words.

One night, I will experience that fear again. She had spent the day with Martine, helping her to prepare her exams. From the back of the apartment, their laughter came to me, the answer to a few moments of relaxation after the long silence of study time. By the end of the afternoon, they had prepared the meal, playing and singing in the midst of the pots and steaks. I wanted to help with the chore but quickly felt excluded from what, when they were together, took a festive air. As Marco was congratulating them for the meal, "Of course, she said, teasing," it's a success, we know how to cook because we are women!" I detested the sound of her voice during those moments, as I detested the glances exchanged with Martine which also excluded me, sent me back to an original sin, that nothing could absolve me from. The next minute, she would become the pal again, the friend who could forgive everything.

She usually left around midnight. I knocked at Martine's door offering to take her back. She shouted, without opening the door, "If you want to make me a little place, I will sleep here!" It was always thus. She would choose her bed according to her fancy of the day, dragging the sofa from the living-room into the room that Marc and Martine shared, or asking me to make her a little space in my bed. I never found out what, during the day, might have directed her choice.

— Eli, you resemble a frog in the middle of digestion!

She was standing at the doorway, standing out against the light of the corridor, smiling sweetly, but because of the allusion I knew she was looking for a fight, provoking me for the fun of it. I answered her softly, "Go take a bath, it's late! I do not accept anyone dirty in my bed tonight!" She closed the door and I thought she was out of the room, but when I looked, I saw the dark mass of her body at the foot of the bed. She was taking off her clothes as usual, carefully putting them down on the table.

— Would you like a towel?

— I will wash up later!

— I was wary of the softness in her voice, closing my eyes in order not to see that she was keeping nothing on, and not putting on the t-shirt, too large, that I had taken out for her as usual. I kept my eyes closed in order not to feel her sliding underneath the sheets, I was still trying to play the game in order not to think about her warmth.

— You are trying to cheat! I said no dirty person in my bed.

I was waiting for her to laugh, the pillow thrown in my face or the discussion she would initiate, looking serious, about the suitable hours for bathing, imitating with her high-pitched voice the schoolteachers of cartoons. But she had got closer, leaning over my chest, placing her right arm on the other side of my body.

— Smell! Do I smell bad? I dare you say I smell bad!

Her voice was still full of laughter! She knew that I did not dare move for fear of brushing against her body. Her body was shaking with laughter! Her mouth was next to my ear and she let herself fall on my chest. There was her smell, her breath, the shape of her breasts and I heard laughter in her voice. I was afraid to move, afraid to answer, afraid of another burst of laughter which would tell me it was a game. She could not be playing at hurting me so!

I had accepted the indifference, the patient discovery of trust, the fragile friendship, the difficulty of sharing her laughter when the memory of her sad

eyes, one stormy night, would resurface; I had accepted to forget her restless body next to me, on certain
nights, fighting in its sleep monsters I had never confronted. I could not fight against this new image. She
felt my confusion and to reassure me, nestled against
me, gently stroking my face. I said "why?" and she
said in a burst of laughter "why not?!" I no longer
wanted to know. I was frightened again and, in spite
of her, I heard myself laughing. Because of her unexpected tenderness, because of the warmth of her skin,
because I sensed her attempts to be in control when
desire made her too vulnerable. I was laughing hearing her laugh! I saw her eyes shining in the dim light,
looking, provoking, measuring out my pleasure. I
closed my eyes and she held out her hand. Come
dance, Eli! I was holding her against me, we were
swinging together, floating on the music. She would
stiffen all of a sudden at a drum roll, and the next
minute became soft against me. She put her arms
around my waist and I let myself be led; she put her
head against my shoulder and let herself be carried
along. She pulled back at times, keeping me away and
looked at me smiling as if she suddenly realized who
I was. Then, she took my hands, placed them around
her neck, lifted hers to my shoulders and put her forehead against mine. We were almost of the same
height. And after the last notes, she stayed a few sec-

onds very close against me to keep us up from a brutal return to the surface.

One evening, much later, during one of our stormy arguments on women's struggles, she became quiet for a moment, looked at me and said ironically:

— Eli, I think I am in love with you, but this has nothing to do with our conversation....

Seated at the table, I attempt, through the written words, to heal my pain, knowing that once expressed, when the pain flowing through my fingers will have caused them to shake, I will be able to try and stand back in order to recover my serenity.

I no longer thought I could still suffer from this attitude! I have known for a long time, I have the daily experience of this cruelty (thoughtless, unintentional, I want to believe it) and yet it hurts. I am back from their house, sad, physically tired by this silent rage that, however, I had promised myself to stifle no longer; but because of Julia, of her look begging me not to make things worse, of the implicit promise of her clenched fist, I once again kept quiet, after realizing that a woman was being trampled on and my anger comes from the fact that it is always women who allow themselves to be trampled on.

Julia has been drawing for years, and during all that time, Fred has been destroying what little confidence she has left: he criticized her drawings, judged them childish by the great master, by the renowned artist and deaf to my encouraging remarks, I see her day by day getting further away from her paints. She loves, however, to create illustrations for children's books, beautifully describing worlds and dream characters which remain shut away in her folders, while he, pretending to push her to really express herself, and do some real painting, he is about to snuff all creativity out of her.

229

Why? Why Julia? I have asked her this question since the very first days of our friendship and I never stop asking her because the answers do not succeed in convincing me, nor her either, to whom her own explanations seem clumsy justifications.

I had observed them at my arrival, discovering their love, moved by the old couple likeness, while guessing the tensions, and I thought then that they expressed a normal malaise because of the discussions that life caused them to postpone for another day. I said nothing. I was waiting for the possibility of a dialogue with them. Very quickly, I understood that it would be impossible with Fred. But with Julia, the thread tied around our hands held out. I was afraid of finding a woman wanting to play, years later, the traditional role of the mother, but Julia had no idea on how to play her role in that story, and in the course of months, without forcing, she came to accept me as a friend. I was becoming a woman. She did not try to see the little girl still in me. However, I had kept from my childhood the habit of the "why?" Why do you let yourself be taken advantage of, Julia? She would say, "Fred is right, I should work harder on my painting, but I don't want to paint the way he does, we do not have the same work rhythm." Tell him that, Julia, don't feel guilty! She would smile, "You will understand one day that the creative act, for some women, is not a priority as it is for men especially when they live together." I protest-

ed, *screaming about the suffocation, blaming her upbringing; she did not get angry, often accepted my tentative explanations, whispering that it was difficult to change in one day. You will be different, Julia would tell me; as for me, I wanted to shake off the too-heavy burden of her habits. When I was afraid to have been too hard on her, I would kiss her, telling her my tenderness for her, reassuring the woman whom my vehemence at times worried. I want you to go too fast Julia, I forget that we do not have the same rhythm, but try to understand me, I have dreamt so much about you that at times I get the different images mixed up. And Julia would listen, smiling, closing her eyes when I would tell her stories about her that I had invented, shaking her head when I would say unacceptable words.*

Julia, why did you leave Paul? Mysterious, she would answer, "I was very young," and one day she will say, "If I had then the maturity of today, I would have never left Paul. But at the time, I judged it unacceptable that he had other women in his life. I did not understand him, Lili, and I think that he did not understand either what was going on with him." Was Paul a womanizer? "Don't put a label him! Not you!" She was right, I had so often told her that I detest preconceived ideas about people, that I am allergic to classifications, especially those they want to affix on me. Besides, it's one of the reasons for my tenderness for Julia: friendship, closed doors, curled up on a bed we talk about the cheerful, the sensible, the sadness and the madness. Julia accepted everything, the contradictions, my sudden infatuations in spite of my tenderness for Michel, my affairs that she envied out loud, my fits of anger against Fred which she understood while keeping her mouth shut, my solitude so far away from everybody when the demons came back. And if she worried about my convictions, she asked no questions. I had freely talked to her, about Romain and his words at our first meeting, "I want you!" How I had laughed at his arrogance! Julia listened. No man will ever own me, no man will ever have a hold over me. Julia would interrupt me then, expressing her fears, her doubts, for it was no longer a theoretical discussion but it was about my relations with very real people and her questioning would then delve back into the different developments. "Aren't you afraid of missing out on love, Lili, aren't you rushing headlong? Perhaps, you want to go too fast, find out too fast. And most of all, I am afraid of something else: I know you, I know that for you security is important, but what about them, aren't they seeing you as an easy girl?" But Julia, I am not looking for anything else but love and I am not easy, on the contrary, I am even very difficult when it's about holding on to my love. She would burst out laughing, knowing that I was ready to say anything in order to pacify her.

There are times when I miss those moments. They

have become much fewer since I have been living far away from her and now, when I go and spend a moment with her, I leave often sad or angry, not having had the time to talk to her and hear her explanations.

Monday, February 18, 197...

Liza,

Two months without writing to you, I do not deserve absolution! I needed your recent angry letter to shake me up.

I do not have to prove to you that I want to keep the bond, you are vexing when you hint at my indifference. I do not want to seek excuses either, they have never been necessary between us. I am only going to explain the commotion of these past two months. Once again, I have changed apartments. With boxes to pack and unpack, space to make livable, the apartment is larger, it was necessary to furnish the extra rooms. I lived in a whirlwind. We did everything: the furniture in the drawing-room, the installation of the new mauve carpets, the new bookcase. I learned to use my hands: with a saw and a hammer, it was a painful training, but the results make me proud. I found it gratifying to do something else than hold a pen, and I am still at it. Don't laugh! It's a fascinating discovery to see my hands moving, my hands creating.

As soon as I feel less rushed, I will write to you at length, and will answer your last two letters.

I have found the collection that you were asking me, I am sending it to you separately. I like this Québécois writer, we could discuss her text after you have read it.

Kisses. Keep writing.

Paul

Kingston, December 26, 197...

Liza,

I received your letter the day I left. You must ask yourself what I am doing here! I found myself, two days before Christmas, on a plane, because I could not do otherwise. This trip was suddenly decided, I did not have the time to talk to you about it.

In fact, it's neither a vacation nor a real trip, but a meeting with Paul. For several months now, Eli and I, we have talked about carrying out our plans of returning home. We feel like spending a first tentative stay there before what we want to be the last Québec move. I had to speak to Paul, see Paul, listen to him because of the time elapsed. Eight years for Eli. Twelve years for me. During those years, we may have turned into adults! ... Years of a different life when we have lived so briefly the real one in our country. The anguish of the return!... How is it possible?

We have been talking a lot for three days, and we listen to Paul. At times, a mad impulse: buy two tickets and go right away to get reacquainted, to spend the New Year with our family. Paul tempts us with stories of the preparations for the holidays. We hesitated until his departure a while ago, but it was not reasonable to do so and in any case Christmas vacation in Haiti is not a daily occurrence. We fly back tomorrow to the deep cold, we are not attracted by this island, we do not want to be tourists and we do not know anyone.

All these discussions with Paul have at once reassured and worried me. Why this desire to return? I have the sensation of thinking too logically, too coldly. I draw a line through anything else existing inside of me, hidden by the smart words I try to form in my head. The doubt subsists, Liza, and I think that I am wrong not to express it. But I am afraid of the answers that I could find. Would I have the courage to accept them, to want to respect what is profoundly hidden? The doubt is already there. I am aware of it, but it is more comforting not to stick to it words that have been uttered...

See you soon,

P.

Patrick

Constantly questioning oneself to get the answers!... Six months of incessant quarrels, in the end I said no to everything Romain wanted to force on me; I had identified what I rejected, the non-desired life, convinced I would detest this world of lies, hypocrisies but I still ignored the strength of my new desires. But what about the rest? In my head I knew, I was full of perfect theories and had to be satisfied with them. Patrick came to sit next to me, and it was enough for him to speak to make me want to know everything about him. The constant proofs! How could I have guessed his fear? I was coming out of a suffocating daily routine, six months of hallucinations, and he maintained that we were alike. I did not see the error! I accepted the distance, to see each other every now and then, nothing more, aware that I wanted this agreement in principle. I learned nothing about his friends, about his former life nor about his thoughts; I ignored his tastes, his troubles, I learned nothing about him, accepting this extreme situation in order to prove to myself I was strong and I learned nothing about myself: he would say, "we each have our life," I know now that he was hiding; he would say "we each have our own friends," I now know his fears. Each of us was alone and I ended up feeling that he did not care about my reality, I learned nothing but the past, idealized in his head by the distance in time and space: the dream country that he created for me, for him and that I ended up rejecting. I still bear the scar of that evening when I understood there existed no friendship between us: this discussion with a friend, useless, and that night, I started to distance myself from his new lies. He did not know anything about me, had not taken the time to get to know me, had not given me the time to discover him. I knew him only in bits and pieces, through cross-checking, and only a taste of cinnamon and the break of that evening remained with me.

Still, the clues were there, everywhere, in the course of our story: his gaze upon me during one festive evening when I had come to my friends' place, not knowing that he would be there, not paying attention to his presence. Already, in the background, Eli was making me dance and laugh all those nights. Patrick was looking at us, and I rejected the questions deep in his eyes "I am going to wait for you outside." No, I don't feel like leaving, not with you, I am not with you. He was outside, in the cold, when I looked out the window and went out to join him. "Which one do you like?" First worry. And our pact? "Curiosity," he said. Eli! He is relieved. He will say, "I feared it might be Marc" and will say sounding ironic, "He is my ex-wife's lover and I would not have appreciated that... This would have been too much."

I detested those words but was unable to interpret the clues. And on my birthday, when sitting next to me, after a glass of rum, "Lili, I love you!" I was furious at those words contrary to our rules, at the pretext to say what was inexpressible. There was no love between us, he was cheating, and I was afraid our pact would suffer the consequences. Should I have renegotiated? I did not want love, I only thirst for open expanses after the painful winter. In the end, he said, "I am leaving soon" and I was waiting for him to leave before organizing my own trip to another continent. But he stayed there, time was passing by, "You will come and join me." I will not come and join you, one day perhaps I will decide to visit this country but not to join you. He lingered in my life, so I decided to speed up the flight. During that summer, I am going to meet Liza and Michel, I am going to discover another woman. Time to be again with Liza.

   She says, "Good morning, I am a friend of your brother" and he smiles. A few days later, she will again say "I am a friend of." Patrick had suggested, before his departure, "If you have any problems, go see my brother," and for days she stays shut in a dark little room. She and her anger at having gotten sick, the need to isolate herself, to take care of herself in her solitude. Liza comes everyday with bread and milk. The young girl lives on bread and milk and in that room that gives her nausea, she cleans to sweat, to move, so as not to feel the revolting pain. Then the nightmare returns! Afterward, she wants to go out, to see the sun in the streets, go to the post office or call him. The telegram sent read "will call, Tuesday 10 o'clock," he answers that it's going to cost him a fortune she could have cared less about it because she needs the sound of his voice, a few words, a laugh in order not to shout her pain. "We will see each other soon, I have again postponed my trip." She believes him, she wants to believe him in order not to think about the pain. She knows those days away from him will be wonderful because of Liza to whom she declares, "If I find him, I will do something drastic!" Patrick is no longer there, she did something drastic: "Julia, in October, I am going to live alone." No one protested then while before there was sadness, refusal; now, nothing because her voice is different, firm. Paul felt ready, wanting a total solitude even at the price of their absence. And the others, he elsewhere, Liza in Paris, now Eli gets on her nerves! Liza would say laughing, "Don't let anyone live with you!" Anybody can live with her, anyone and everyone has at times settled in her life, but she keeps her crazy girl's head. It's with Patrick that she started to think about it: I am on the path that must lead to understanding, serenity, and every pain is a step on this path. In the streets, she sometimes sees a face that has crossed her life, but she has forgotten, only life experience counts! She often recognizes faces without names, and names without faces. Total oblivion. Those hands of one day, of one night, the time of a weekend in New York, but this wound is still bleeding. Steve, whom she must have hurt! She regrets nothing. He was sleeping, there was the other one, she was cold that night, nothing could muddle her mind. She had tried to keep the bond, he has never answered. No matter, she did not feel any bruising. At her return, she spoke about it only to the one who said he understood everything. She only talked about the horrible, the painful part, the rape! It was a rape, Eli, even though it didn't leave any physical marks. He used my dreams, spoke about our rage, he took the right to want my body because of our shared madness. This girl who was seeking a friend, who thought she had found a brother, he heard none of her screams, he understood nothing about her mute suffering, because he only looked at her breasts, only wanted to experience her sex. She was ashamed in spite of all the books having conditioned her. She said, "I detested him that day in New York." Later, she refused to see him in spite of his incessant requests, at first she would answer "I am sick" and in the end, she stopped answering him. One day someone told her about his first-born child, she remained indifferent. She should have perhaps spoken to him, explained to him her disappointment, the girl who believed in the difference! She should have screamed, "You, who think like me, who at least say it, who wrote on this page the end of a poem that I had start-ed for fun and your spouse so close to us.... But she was waiting in the drawing-room while you were rap-ing me. Did she know that I was dying next door when, with her hand on her stomach, she was feeling the heartbeats of your child?" I did not want to see the shame in her eyes, I did not want to see the shame in my eyes. Would she have protested if I had screamed? I hope so even though I did not trust her at the time.

Listen to me, I was not looking for absolution! Once more, I noted that his beautiful words did not mean respect for all. I know, I am a woman but you will admit with me that he would not have screwed a man, whom he would have felt close to, the way he screwed me. So I am not a human being because I am a woman? You could not care less about it, I can feel it, but I will not stop. I did not have the courage to discuss it in New York, nor with Liza in Paris. I did not have the courage to call out for help; would Liza have detested this woman who was drowning? A woman does not have the right to say no. I made myself a promise, it's the last time. Do you hear me?

The last time!

He is looking at her smiling and he says, "Come, I want you." She starts screaming.

❧

The nightmare. I am seated, I speak: lots of words one after the other and the sound of my voice surprises me! Metallic, unusual rhythm, jolts, havoc! He looks at me, listens, I know that he does not hear me. Somewhere in his head, he is timing the continuation of this moment. I am already afraid, without knowing what exactly is going to happen. Without knowing? Why did I talk about New York, last night? I keep on talking to him. The room is becoming ever more tiny and dark, and I am lying down, sick on this narrow bed. I said, "No, I don't want to! Why did you accept my desire before and do not recognize my right to talk about its absence?" I don't want to, he knows it, I told him so. He also knows that she is close by, that I would like to call out to her. But he smiles. So he knows about a woman's fear, a woman's shame! Where did he learn that I would not be able to stand the gaze of that other woman? I am lying down on this gray cover, she is within earshot, accessible to love and I do not trust the love of a woman. Again, I try to speak. I cannot even cry, hatred settling in me hurts me too much. I will not succeed in forgetting that he is going to destroy years of understanding for this moment, his moment of pleasure. I said no and he refused to hear me. A nightmare in which for the last time, he was the stronger. And I was not sleeping.

Leaning against the wall of the old building, silent and motionless, she draws long breaths, feeling her heart rushing all over the place. She, it is me, this woman breathless because she has been racing, a question of life and death, throughout the streets of the neighborhood. She has never been afraid of death, but this insult, these words that she still hears seemed to her worse than a knife stabbing her in the back. And after her reaction, he went on, "Whom do you take yourself for?" For nothing! But it was the start of the malaise. The other one, without a word, listened to them tearing each other apart, and did not react to the cruel words. She decided to leave, to run away, to no longer hear those words that were still resonating. Outside, winter and her race to the wall, against which, breathless, she leans in order never to die. The beginning of the malaise which will make her leave to never come back, to go and find Liza and Michel, in order to forget. "If you are in trouble, call my brother, he lives in Paris." She knows it's their last meeting, they will never see each other again, but he does not know it yet. At once sad and tender, love for the last time. She will retain for a long time the memory of his body, but not the taste. "You taste of cinnamon." I could not care less for the taste of cinnamon, I would have preferred real friendship, loyalty.

Running far away to regain my balance, forget that he was looking, impassive, at a woman suffering. We will see each other again, he says, when she talks of leaving, you will come and see me soon, next summer. She did not answer. She hopes that in the meantime, she will have found other habits and will forget the smell of his pipe. On the plane, she fell asleep looking at a film.

It's already spring! Coming home tonight, I raised the storm windows to let in the air still cold at the onset of the season. The apartment is not as dark. I stay there, in the pleasing half-light, sitting on a cushion in the drawing-room, waiting for Claudine's arrival and postponing the moment of preparing the meal. My friend is aware of my lack of culinary enthusiasm, and on the phone yesterday, she had expressly said she would help me. She knows I do not rush to the stove, as soon as I get home. I love too much these moments of quiet solitude between the hustle and bustle of the metro and the noise of the entrance door that Eli opens. I think I am pregnant and I am hesitant to talk about it yet, fearing the disappointment of those Christmas days, when my being a little late had made Eli and Julia jump for joy. I am waiting to be sure because these little stomach cramps could explain my being two months late. I must make an appointment at the hospital. I will also have to carefully read the Union policy on maternity leave. These concerns irritate Eli who claims that I do not have to pay attention to those details. And why, working in a particular environment, should I pretend to be different, elsewhere, to have no benefits in a situation when women are often penalized?

Once again, our last argument comes to my mind. I, living in this country, refusing to always be outside of this life, participating in the lively atmosphere of the office, in the creation of a women's group, accepting the responsibility of a voting booth for municipal elections, I try to explain to Eli the importance of my participation. But, he only reiterates his refusal to get involved. Both of us were nervous, using hurtful words to express our different perceptions, options. The trip planned for this summer, our discussions on the reasons for this introductory trip did not contribute to help us regain our serenity. The tone of voices would often rise and I would scream, Don't provoke me! I feel you are, just like me, tense, waiting for this trip to be over with and hoping for positive results. You are having fun at getting me upset, you will end up succeeding! It's true that I am worried. It's just that my experience of this wintry country has been different from yours. So what? You claim that I have adapted marvelously well, I refuse to hear the word assimilated. You know very well that I could not be. I love life here, I have gotten used to the fall, I can withstand the long winters, I have adjusted the rapid pace to my personal rhythm, at times, charging and at others nonchalant, I know when to make the necessary pause, and without calming down my urgencies, I have created a space to slow down which goes countercurrent to the feverish agitation of those who do not know when to stop when the moment of effective action is gone. I have found, in this city, realities and people that at the present time suit me and when comes the time to leave for good, because it will come, I will have a hard time leaving them.

I have made friendships, regardless of what you think, those bonds are very strong. You refuse the gesture, unable to admit, that at times it was up to you to take the first steps, you, however, who knows the sweetness of an outstretched hand. They have learned only mistrust and isolation while you have lived in the open, with doors wide open all day long, a life in the open air where others see and wait for you to look at them, and their looks often made you angry.

Here, you have closed yourself to all contact, you have chosen to live as if you were not in this country. You had told me, do you remember, it was at the beginning of our story, that I was the one you wanted to return home with. I understood, while avoiding your bad faith. I could have answered you that, living elsewhere, you therefore did not wish to share your life here with me! I am exaggerating, I know! You were offering me your dream and your hopes, but I feel comfortable here, I want to feel comfortable where I am and not live with my head elsewhere. I refuse to constantly live in transit, neither here nor in our homeland.

Soon, we will go back. Our story, which began with this sentence of yours that I accepted as a mark of trust, is linked to the Return. The difference between us is that I will really return, leaving behind habits, loves, places where I have learned to live, in spite of the pain of the separation. You will come out of the nightmare of this interlude that you did not live and you will have wasted eight years of consciousness, for you know very well that these years have marked you in spite of yourself.

You claim that the best part was possible for me because of my skin color. Easy, Eli, too easy. I have told you that for me, this reality has never been important, neither at home, nor here and you reproached Paul not to have taught me such a shared and widespread weakness in our world. I reject your criticisms. Paul has never taught me that skin shades could be important, it's true! but I was not unaware of certain cruel realities linked to the epidermis. Paul did not allow me to internalize racism as a component of my personality but, very early, I understood that it existed everywhere. Still, I have never winced upon hearing them talk about me as "the little black girl at the office." Your interpretation is dishonest: if I have a different experience due to my skin color more or less dark, then no discussion is any longer possible. I am like that and the "if I were different" will not solve our argument.

Above all, I do not want you to try and destroy

these twelve years, not in the name of the racism of those people from here. I have met many an ignorant person, just like you, but I have also met the others, my friends that I will leave behind with tears in my eyes and for whom I will keep my affection.

∂∞∂

The pain around my forehead, the presence of the body that does not sleep. She feels this body and the impression of knowing it already: the fever of the earlier days in the house with the blue room. Everything is spinning, noises go fast; she doesn't know how to describe it to those who hurt like her, she cannot explain this spinning in her head. Who wants to have her believe in evil? She would like the noise to go on. The difference of feeling oneself living through an unpleasant sensation of non-reality. Transformed, distorted, emptiness inside, life all around! The smells no longer correspond with the days of throbbing migraines, sweet smells of the evening nights going all the way up the Atlantic to this cold gray land that summer does not succeed in warming up. The City! City of indifference and oblivion where anonymity is not the calm and joy of feeling ignored but the violence of the gaze, the violence of the feigned insouciance, of the false and exaggerated interest to mask the panic in front of the other one. She feels this slow burning aggression and the madwoman in her head would like to tell of the tenderness at times, the happy discoveries but the mind does not want to remember. The choice of not turning away from the anger for a hand stretched out, one hand alone and one smile alone for hundreds of stolen looks. No!... One must speak of the softness of those whose mute question does not need an answer. Weariness healed in the arms of the children of this dull city! To forget the pain, once memory is erased, and to accept the happiness of hurting on leaving them one day, soon. Knowing what is missing because of a knowing smile, the sorrow of losing them after having looked after them for so long. And finally to understand that one must forget.

Montreal, June 22, 197...

Liza,

I have not written to you for several weeks now because I was unable to do so.

I lost my baby. Hospital, pain... I will be convalescing for several weeks.

If you can, call me. I will try to tell.
Love
P.

Port au Prince, August 15, 197...

Liza,

You will not read these pages for a few weeks. I had thought of writing to you at the end of my trip to tell you about my impressions, the reunions, and the first night of my arrival, I open this notepad for a travel diary that is addressed to you. Later, you will know how I became reacquainted with this place and those people that I left such a long time ago.

Today, I could not sort things out or so little! The arrival, the first shock of those shantytowns around the airport, the joy to hug the ones I love and also the first tensions that I thought had disappeared. Paul wanted us with him, Marie also, and once more I found myself caught in between the two of them.

We are presently in her home. Still, I would have preferred to spend my stay at Paul's. I have so many things to tell him.

Montreal, September 12, 197...

I should have known that my plan of keeping a diary would not work out. Three weeks, it's brief and I did not take the time to write, to jot down my thoughts. Meetings, the family, a few old acquaintances and some rare friends — and visits to places I was rediscovering. Most of all Paul and his words, Paul and his dreams! It's possible, he says, everything is possible! I believe him. I hope it's true. I feel less anguish at the thought of returning to live here. (You see I am already saying here when I am thinking of over there!) Paul is here and this matters a great deal to me.

I don't know why, but this trip seems to me the outcome of a cycle. The last trip, the last vacation. When do I have the right? Why this idea of right? I do not think this thought is exclusively linked to an economic reality which, I know, will be more precarious but I ignore what brought it on. Since my return from vacation, I invest all of my energy in the preparations for the last trip. It will not take a long time, a few months! The time to put aside enough money to hold on the first months, while avoiding all unnecessary expenses, leaving the apartment two or three months before the trip in order to save on the rent. We have decided to sell everything, the furniture, the car, and keep only the strictly necessary.

I end here. I am tired.

You are very much in my thoughts,

Kisses,

P.

Lucie

What a program! You have no idea what you were exposing yourself to?... To tell you about women... I couldn't tell you about women, but rather about my women; those who fill my heart and my life, those who, as accomplices, respect my strength and bolster my faltering steps, those who are friends, those who share, those who nurture and want me wise, and those wild ones who protect my bursts of laughter, my marvelous women whom I wear around my heart.

Marie-the-tenderness, who wants to mother me and whom I call Auntie Ma because I say "Mommy" only with great difficulty; Julia who does not belong to any category besides, I don't ever put my women in a mold, Julia who knows to listen to me as well as to offer me her incomplete words, shameless Julia who accepted to be my daughter in the daytime and who, at nightfall, sang lullabies to a Lili now all grown up. This was mostly during the times of flight. I experienced those evenings as so many pretexts, as so many justifications for a need to let my hair down. I spent certain nights next to you to forget the fear, to put to sleep my devouring demons and, in the morning, I felt that this drug did not have any lingering effects. You did not understand my about-faces, you interpreted my sudden rejections, you could not hear the pressing call. After a period of foolish running around, I would invoke the name of Julia whom you did not dare stand against. And, sincere, I would go to her. For the tenderness, to continue with another kind of headlong flight. Those days, those nights besides her, a break, a pause between the happy excitation in the midst of the tribe, and my retreats, were full of laughter and whispers. Julia the friend with whom I enjoyed the sweetness of woman talk, Julia and the intonations of regret in her voice telling me about her painful experience when I spoke of the new life which enthused me. She knew how to listen to my first faltering steps without playing the guide or the censor, expressed her surprise at my lucidity, marveled at my rage for autonomy, and lulled my multiple heart and body pains. Julia my mother, whose certain gestures reminded me of Jeanne whom I am unable to forget although she is so far away from my life. I don't write to Jeanne, I do not receive from her any news of our life together, and yet, I know that the bond endures because I love Carole, and I am worried about Annie who is growing up. "Aunt Ma, please be patient with my little sister!" I would love to see Annie again and also Rachel too young at the time of the green house to have been a friend like Carole, and too old now to be my little sister, like Annie. I often feel guilty not to be close to them, as I am with Monique and Ginou, furious at being used as their shield, their role model, happy to see myself being treated as undesirable object. I am the old fogey, and the accomplice, petted affectionately at times, rejected at others. Annie and Rachel will not know this game so different from *Tibobo Pépé,* and at my return, I may not be able to regain the tenderness which made them smile with happiness and pride when in the morning, troublemakers that we were, we went to school, a rope tied around their waists, Carole and I holding the ends, happy to shock the good folks.

I have told you before about Claudine, I have shared with you the evenings with Claudine now. Martine is between us in spite of the gentleness that you so often felt excluded from. And Liza! I am still unable to tell you about Liza, I can only promise you another trip, another continent, to meet Liza. Will I be able to describe Lucie adequately to you?

The first day, she was standing on a restaurant table visibly drunk, singing loudly a Quebecois folk song. All around her, the office colleagues, the employees who came from different regions and companies, the waitresses and the clients who entered there by accident, all of them were looking at her reprovingly, waiting for the stumble that would do her in, her legs and inspiration altogether gone. I walked up to her and offered her my hand which she took with a taunting smile, and I made her step down slowly. Her stride was confident in spite of the four bottles of beer she walked around while singing. That first day was a Friday afternoon, she followed me home and spent the entire weekend in my apartment.

I had already held my hand out to others that year when I was learning real life: Louise, cheerful, very beautiful and full of complexes, wanting to be loved for herself and not for her blue-green eyes. She had attacked me from the very first instant of our friendship: "Women do not love me because I am beautiful and men because of it." I had teased her to dissipate the misunderstandings: "You know, I am from another culture, my criteria for beauty are different from yours, different from the criteria of the people here, to me your face looks like those of all the women I come across. I do not want to hurt your feelings but it's impossible for me to find white people beautiful." She laughed to tears, we have been able to find the right words to maintain the friendship. When Mado decided to tell us about her dreams for a new life, I found out that I had two friends: the beautiful one who is too beautiful and the little redhead crazy about ecology.

There was also Marisa, whose humor froze my friends when, with her voice of good little girl, she threw at them in the midst of a discussion about men and women, "You and I we understand one other, we love women in the same way!" Marisa so fragile behind her provocative mask. And Simone whom I do not need to make you discover, her presence in my life will resist even the distance. Simone, my sister here in spite of the different realities and culture. With them, I suddenly discovered the presence of women in my life. Not only one woman with whom the bond had become very strong, not only with Julia and Liza, but women for all seasons: discussions, parties, affection, anger, laughter, misunderstandings, friendship, loyalty and madness. Women were in my life and I accepted them as they were. I saw that the little girl who had only male friends because girls were busy with frivolous concerns, because girls had a habit of tearing each other apart, because, in truth, the girls I met had not had the opportunity to take an interest in anything but make-up and gossip; I became aware that the little girl that they called a tomboy had become a woman and had joined women. The only one missing was my lost puppy and Lucie began to sing on the table of the restaurant.

At first, our friendship will consist of words: she would talk about what ailed her, and I would comfort, insult or amuse her. Her life was falling apart because of a man, my life then forced her to laugh. When she cried, when I felt she was too depressed, I would promise to refuse visiting Eli, so that one of those mean men would be punished in turn. When Phillipe would not come home three days in a row, I would break up with my lover of the month and she would scream at me, "You are crazy!", laughing hysterically. We were both crazy, she for having become too attached, and I for refusing all ties in the name of survival. And the day when I saw her eyes shine looking at Pierre, I organized a party during which I fell asleep in order to let them write the beginning of their story.

You had asked me, curious and surprised, what united me to a woman like Lucie who seemed to you so different from me and I answered you, "Why not?" Why should I love only the women who resemble me? I took the time to know the woman I had held my hand out to in a noisy restaurant. It could have happened that Lucie and I might not have gotten along, but not because of our dissimilarity. After comforting my lost puppy, after Pierre's arrival, the mothering period over, we started the giving and taking of friendship. I dragged her along to the parties of March 8th, asking her to sing our songs, she spoke to me of metaphysics causing me to panic when she showed me what she called my gift as a medium. I was next to her during this strange, unexplained contact with Paul and it was her turn to reassure me. "It's normal, don't worry, you heard his voice across hundreds of kilometers because he needed you, he was thinking about you during a moment of anguish; in fact, there are no other words, he was calling you and you heard. Don't look for logical and rational explanations, scientists will find it later. Just be happy you heard him." I was afraid, it's true. So what? It was not enough for me to distance myself from her. Not her enthusiasm for astrology, not her adorable quirks as a vegetarian not her intransigence of a non-smoker! I don't smoke in her home, and I give up eating meat around her and she does not get angry when I tease her about her astronomical maps. It does not cost me anything to respect her choices, no contradiction tears me up, and I know she likes following me in my reflections on the difficult autonomy, and during my visits at the women's bookstore. When she gets taken in, I am there; when in the name of freedom I strike blindly, she reminds me of the importance of love. We are different, Eli, and she felt like having her hair curled to please me, as for me I have started to wear light dresses because she detested my jeans. We were different but we loved each other.

Lucie was the first one to stay in my apartment with the mauve carpets, you will come later and one day you will sneak off leaving the place to Paul, who used to frighten you. Do you remember the trip when I met Gina, her friend that I wanted immediately to love and to whom I gave the first pages of the text: You came back after their departure.... There is room for a lot of people in my apartment, there's room for all of those I love in my life, even if they are not like me.

☙

The days of scorching sunshine, the visions will be back, I promise you. We will know again the despondency of the great summer heat. Do not listen to the others who tell you to give up. I shut my ears to the discouragement, I refuse to see their hopeless faces, I do not look for any precise limits, it would hurt too much when the date came and went. No! I feel full of fears, and yet, I still believe, I want to believe until the end of my night. I am building my life on this great madness even if those for whom I keep a remnant of affection do not understand my stubbornness. They call me by all these strange names which no longer scare me. No matter the letters or the words that surround me, no matter how they qualify my superb folly, I promise you, we will tremble again during the days of strong winds, we will live through new cyclones. We are used to hurricanes. Rain does not scare us. I believe in the sun beating on the heads of those who have never known gentleness. In the meantime, I will survive. I survive until the next upheaval. I have told you the story, I do not know the rest, but I predict the end. We will have a girl who will resemble you, I repeat to all those who bore me with their preconceived ideas that I will not be a mother. It's true, I want to become a mother in the devouring fire, I want this daughter who will be the child of all those who have kept their hands wide open. This daughter of mine, I will bear her for those who will not be able to have any; and if I can't I will bring her into the world pulling her out of the wombs of a thousand women to celebrate the new day. Later, we will let the children discover by themselves. We will not tell them about the pain, our eyes will speak for us!

I spent the evening in their company. There is sadness in their looks, but they show their impassive faces to my panic-stricken eyes; they, my quiet loves for whom I laughed a little to recreate the cheerful mood. But the shadow is there, this departure, and I felt that the wait was worse than the apparent insouciance. I ran away! I went home alone, between four walls, curled into a ball and listened to my silences and the dull sound of this stranger in my chest. I suddenly feel the need to destroy the calmness of this intrusive silence, I feel that my head is too heavy. Even if I no longer find my deft fingers, all of a sudden, in this enclosed space, I allow my right hand to play at the adult. I write to conjure up my lot. I feel a vortex in the pit of my stomach and this violence scares me. I am no longer able to repress it. I knew, a long time ago, how to live with it, how to reach a compromise in order not to lose my balance; today, it takes the entire place left by the emptiness. I do not want to let myself be fooled. They and the tenderness that dulled my fears as if I was under the effect of a soporific. However I was not lying, I looked at my anesthetized self. One must not accept suffocation in this web woven by others, I refuse the saying made-up by charlatans: Happy people do not have a story. Then, we will not have a story? They lied. It's about finding a story that matches the size of the revolt, even if the doubt of the past threatens the balance, this doubt that tore me from the comfort of tenderness, the days I could no longer take it. And the violence has come back to me! And yet, I feel that I would like to tell with other words, with another language, of this explosion which must occur: to tell how everything will have happened, to tell why I will stop writing for years, because I will stop for a while, when I will no longer have the time, it will belong to others. I must learn to forget the dull pulsations of my blood, to close my eyes, to shut my ears, when the soporific tenderness comes.

– pause.

Winter is already here. In the excitement of the preparations, I did not feel it coming. For a few days now, I wake up each morning hoping to discover on the windowsill a few snowflakes announcing the first snow- falls. It has not snowed yet and I think that I will not see it this year, the dancing of these fluffy balls under the beams of the pale sunrays. Why this regret, this sadness, when the reality of these past twelve years has taught me that it rarely snows before Christmas. How many Christmas Eve revels have we prepared, anxious , fever- ish, waiting for the snow to fall, hoping that when we got out at midnight our coats would be overlaid with this thin icy pellicle. Julia, Monique, Ginou and I, forgetful of the sunny Christmases of our country, could no longer imagine a Christmas Eve revel other than enveloped in the whiteness of a winter frost. I will soon have to re- accustom myself to the torrid heat of a 24th of December in the dusty streets of downtown Port au Prince.

I turn in circles in the empty apartment, looking at the surroundings where I have lived during the past few months. We have decided to sell everything, includ- ing the furniture built with much laughter and clumsi- ness. I only want to hold on to the memories: the rug of my Mexican trip, the lampshades made during lunch time with the girls, the paintings given by Paul, these dishes chosen at the time of the first mauve apartment, memories already in pointillés. And, of course, the most important, the only objects which I would not easily get rid of, or leave voluntarily behind, my books, already for a week now, put in boxes piled up along the entrance wall. These books will be the only complete relic of all these years: Montreal, May 10, 1975 - Paris, July 1978 - and again, and again, I will know how to retrace the erased itinerary. I realize all of a sudden that a second past is about to exist, although I have not yet made a complete inventory of the first, Lili's past. For twelve years, I have been Paul and I do not know which name is going to stick to me once I step down from this plane – the tickets have been bought a long time ago and are lying on my desk. Paul exists, Lili escapes me, still. Pause.

Tonight, I am of all the nightmares and all the solitudes. When I shut myself in, the walls around me do not matter much. I close my eyes and this child humming in the last light of a day about to die, comes back to me. Why she? Why tonight, in a closed room, do I find again this girl that I no longer recognize? The house is large, she had the choice, and yet she had decided on this open space, on the roof of the garage, there was her place of confinement. She would stay there for hours, under the sun, at times, more often at the approach of the night, creating blown out worlds and humming this haunting tune. For the country.... For the ancestors.... Why this tune? Why those silent words? Paul worried about her

isolation in a dangerous spot, about this wanted reclusion. In the room of the well-heated apartment, I often experience the marvelous solitude of the roof of the green house. On some evenings, tired of waiting, he would ask the little girl to get in, holding out his hand which she would take with trepidation. What if he let go of her?

— Three stars from the corner of my eye. I do not want to open the right eye, the sky will become too big. I keep three stars at the edge of the left eye. If I open my eyes wide, I will be over-starred.
— After I count three hundred stars, if Paul calls me, he will be nice to me.

I did not work as hard as he would have liked me to this term. I did not feel like studying, even less like being attentive in class. The only moments of the day that I like are those I spend here, in my house with the open sky above, alone, waiting for Paul's voice which will call through my walls of silence. I know that he worries, he doesn't like knowing that I am on the rooftop of the house. He is particularly afraid of the route, jumping from the balcony on to a piece of the sloping roof over the gallery and, from there, diving toward the roof of the garage.
This spot belongs to me. No one comes here. Without words, there has been an agreement: this place is

not to be violated! When it's still daytime, I go up to read or write in my house; at night, I look at the stars and I sing. Paul detests hearing me sing standing underneath the stars. I try not to do it any longer since he explained to me that it bothers him, but I cannot always stop myself; some nights, it's stronger than I, I sneak out of the room where my three sisters sleep and I climb back to my starry roof. Other nights, the nightmare comes back, and I can no longer move.

This nightmare, I have it again, haunting, for many nights. A man enters the little room in the green house. I am the only one who hears him, in spite of his silent steps, holding his breath. I lose consciousness for a while (seconds, minutes, hours?) Why? I don't know what this man wants because the fear alone exists, my fear, keeping me from the horror. And I stop the unwinding of the conscience. After I come back to reality, I still feel the presence, and the desire to scream comes at last over-whelmingly. I open my eyes, he is there, leaning on me, drawing up the sheet on my shoulders. Paul's face blends with the man's face. I begin to cry. – pause.

The last day in the office. Pauline has handed me my work certificate before my departure this afternoon and I felt everything started to become real. My letter of resignation, the training of my replacement, the sad looks of my closest colleagues, everything seemed to be a bad joke that I was going to dismiss with a laugh: it's over my friends, I was not serious, forgive me this stupid game, I will not do it again. Letter in hand, the game is over. I am about to leave them, I am going away. – pause.

They just left. It's strange this impression of a women's gathering when I know that there were men among us, Eli... Marc... Gérard.... They were drowned in the warmth of my friends from whom I will soon be far away. It's already daylight and the presence still palpable around me of these women that I love has taken me back to the little dancer. A circle of women, in which I immersed myself several hours every day. The little dancer, this skinny child whose reflection I observe in the mirrors which line an entire wall of the big room. She is at the center, other children look at her, leaning against the bars. She stops in the middle of a pirouette. The music continues and the little dancer does not move. The dance teacher waits a few seconds and signals her. She starts over. A few movements. New stop.

— Lili what's wrong?

— I don't feel well. I would like to go home, Madame.

Her face is tense. The teacher agrees and is already waving at another student.

Lili leaves the room and goes toward the locker room. She walks slowly, the feeling persists. She refuses to believe it, but in her head, her father's words "soon, in a year or two, maybe less you will be..." he had spoken to her of.... One evening, he had taken her on his lap and had spoken to her at length about her body, about the changes that had already begun and about those to come. She takes off her leotard and her tights, discovers the humid spot on her clothes before seeing her reddened thighs. Two months ago, she had shown Paul brown spots on her white underwear. He had smiled "It will not be like that every month, it will be heavier, longer too, three or four days," she had not wanted to believe him. Those few brown spots had not bothered her while this hot liquid that she feels running down her thighs disconcerts her. She would have liked to know why. Why? She has heard Paul's voice, she knew the reasons given by science, but in her head the question persists. Why today, when she felt in great shape, when she had practiced so much, why did this blood stop her from continuing with her pirouette? – pause.

I left the apartment four days ago, and this morning, for obscure reasons, under the pretext of a farewell, I went back to this place which still tugs at my heart. I cannot stand seeing this man living in my home. I still say in my home, not able to free myself from these curtains and mauve carpets, from this climbing plant that I watched growing for five years, in this large bed in which I slept alone for a long time and later with Eli. Only Eli! The story is ironic. This man who's going to live in my home will have never lived close to me, with me, the agreement was formal and there it is that Patrick is going to sleep in my bed. He is a stranger whose presence I detest in these premises. – pause.

I have just hung up and his voice still echoes in my ears, tender words, vague worry quickly repressed that I guessed at the cracks, at the sudden breaks, at the sound of an unusual inflection. He knows that we are coming in sixteen days and I realize that I can no longer back out. The recklessness and their possible, probable consequences move all of a sudden to the background. Only the memories surge back and I do not know which ones are the most painful: those twelve years spent here that it will be impossible for me not to retain, in part at least, in brief images, in spite of my capricious memory, or the years from before, from over there, the time of non-memory? – pause.

Montreal July 6, 198...

Liza,

Again, the excitement around me, especially my own activities kept me from writing. The decision is taken, in a few days (I even begin to count the hours) we are going back home. I have already handed in my resignation at the office, sublet my apartment, shipped my "souvenirs" by boat and I am waiting. I feel feverish, anxious without finding a valid explanation to my fear. I will not write much to you today. Maybe in a few weeks, when I will be more or less settled. Write to me to keep the bond, so that I can feel you close to me.

I think about you. A lot.

Soon,

Love

Lili

I am at the end of my rope: visits, conversations, waiting. I can't stand it any more! And this need to look back at the pages. I had decided days ago that this text was finished, that symbolically, this decision coincided with the approach of my departure, and I felt like seeing once more the manuscript buried under my jeans and my t-shirts in the little blue suitcase. Will I be able one day to return to those sentences? I don't know what awaits me, I don't know what I will find over there, what will become of me. I only know that I will lug these pages along with me, as long as necessary. For the exorcism. Tomorrow, I am going away. – Pause?

Interviews with Jan Dominique

(Pointe-à-Pitre, Guadeloupe, May 15, 1997; June 13, 2002)

IF: We will start, if you don't mind, with a classic question. What is your background? Your profession? You are a writer as well as a journalist and the director of Radio Haïti?

JD: I was born and raised in Port-au-Prince where I did all my schooling, primary and secondary up to and including the *baccalauréat*. In those days, in 1970, the Haitian *baccalauréat* was considered valid, therefore I went straight to the University of Montreal... After the university in Montreal, oddly enough I did not get involved in teaching but in trade unionism which fascinates me... The working world was a great discovery for me, a world that had nothing to do with literature and writing. After 1979, I went home; I had decided to stay there and that's when I started to work in the fields of education, literature and journalism. I stayed in the field of education until 1986. In 1986, when the radio station reopened after the fall of the dictatorship, I left it to devote myself almost exclusively to the radio...

IF: I read somewhere that, when you came home to Haïti, the manuscript of *Memoir of an Amnesiac*, your first book, was almost completed...

JD: Yes, the manuscript was completed. Well, I had finished it but it was not published, so I reworked it a little. In Haïti, there are no publishing houses and I did not want to send it elsewhere. I must confess that this idea did not even cross my mind at the time. When I learned there was a literary competition, the *Prix Littéraire Deschamps*, I submitted my manuscript under a pseudonym as I feared two things. At the time, my father was in exile: so, on a political level, the reality was that everyone knew I was his daughter and, since he was in exile, I told myself: "If they know who I am two reactions are possible, either they will worry and not judge my work for what it is worth because the author is the daughter of Jean Dominique, or, on the contrary, my work will draw more attention and enjoy a favorable prejudice." So, I told myself I would use a pseudonym; in this way the work would be judged without reference to the person. Then, I found out that, when the members of the jury chose my book for the literary prize, they wondered who was the author and, as the pseudonym I used was not a Haitian name, they thought the writer was from Quebec!" [laughs] It was then, at that time, that I made it known who I was. Next, the book was published...

IF: You first received the prize and the book was published afterwards!?

JD: That's the prize, in Haiti! It is so difficult to publish a book! The prize is the publication and it continues to be like that.

IF: I was most impressed by the cover of *Memoir,* which is really fantastic, an extraordinary effect of reality. So, I keep wondering, when I look at it, how it was designed.

JD: The cover was designed by a Haitian painter named Ralph Allen. It's a collage that he created. I need to tell you that Ralph is a friend of mine and that he has known me since I was ten. The publishing house had its own graphic artist, so when I decided I wanted a special cover, very nicely I told them it was a book close to my heart and that I really wanted to choose its cover. I asked Ralph: "Would you like to do the cover?" I gave him the manuscript. He said to me: "Fine, I may or may not read it but that's not important." And he created this collage. He told me he had created it from the memories he had of me as a child, therefore he had not read the book. He did not think it was an autobiography and at the limit it was not important for him. What was important was to have complete freedom. He made a collage, he chose, if you want, to walk the same path I had walked, to go to his memory, his recollections of me, things in fact I had completely forgotten. He told me: "When I think of you, I see this picture of a little girl, with her arms open, almost dancing." It's a picture that stayed with him because I often walked to school and literally danced along the way. And he told me: "I very often saw you, when I went by, walking down the sidewalk of the Champ de Mars avenue dancing along." Thus, his own universe met mine.

IF: Shall we speak of the reception of *Memoir of an Amnesiac*? Some critics have judged the text too autobiographical, a commentary I find somewhat ill-founded for two reasons because, in my opinion, when one writes, one rearranges facts and ideas and the whole thing then becomes a creation; I also told myself: "Hum, it's a criticism often made when women write."

JD: Ah, yes, that's what people think right away! Always when it is a female writer, always about women's testimonies, as if women were flawed and could speak only about themselves. People wanted at all costs this narrative to be autobiographical. In fact, what happened with *Memoir*, is that I used from my autobiography what in my judgment were key elements. I needed a base. What counted for me was the literary aspect, for example the story my grand-mother had told me about the child and the Americans. I do not know whether it was true, I have no proof it was true, that was literature. To read that the protagonist had three different mothers but one father only, that for certain people was a real drama. For me, it was a source of creation, just like the story of the little girl and the street vendor of *surettes* (candies) who saves her life.

IF: I loved that passage where the vendor of *surettes* (candies) risks his life for the little girl, during a shooting between government troops and members of the opposition. It's a passage both moving and beautiful, first from a sentimental point of view, because when I was young, I could not do without *surettes*, pistachios and *frescos*, and thus I spent long moments in the company of vendors in front of the school gates. And then, I found this passage moving, because, if one knows Haitian culture well or at least the class divides in the Haitian society, it's truly a remarkable scene.

JD: That's exactly what I wanted to show. You see, what was important for me was of course to show in this passage the violence a child is forced to see; it was also to show that, in this country, in spite of the class divide, this violence can create a solidarity between classes that, otherwise, would have never met. The little girl may be traumatized by such an event but it may also make her discover the vendor of *surettes* who is a wonderful man!

IF: Ah yes! Let's discuss also another passage in the book, that of the slap given to Lili by a father she adores because she had stared at a *macoute*, a slap mentioned throughout the book like an obsession. This passage both struck and surprised me as in the Haitian society, at least in the one I grew up, a child was only slapped for extremely serious offenses. The face is sacred, so this slap, you used it as another literary technique, didn't you?

JD: Absolutely. Children are not slapped in Haiti. She could have been whipped, that's normal. Therefore, when I asked myself what could be the most terrible punishment a father or a mother could inflict upon a child if the child had transgressed certain codes, that's the first thing that came to my mind. I asked myself what could this punishment be for a Haitian child... and I told myself that, if a parent had to make a child realize the danger of the spoken word in a dictatorial regime, what could make an impression on a child was to be slapped... Nowadays, for example, are children slapped in Haiti? Absolutely not! One does not touch the face of a child, it's the most horrible thing a parent can do.

IF: This in a society in which corporal punishment is so common!! Because staring at the *macoute* could lead to her death and I remember that, when I was a young girl in Haiti, I kept my eyes lowered and never looked at people in the eyes.

JD: And certainly not at a *macoute*!

IF: Jan, what literary works have influenced you? What prompted you to write? Who is your favorite writer, what is your favorite work?

JD: Irline, I cannot tell you what has influenced me in literature because I have the ability to read very fast and because I read everything that falls into my hands; I have no preconceived idea in literature, novels, history, science-fiction, detective novels, etc... I started writing very early, around the age of thirteen due to the fact that, since my very early childhood, I have loved to read. I grew up in the midst of a family that read a lot and had a private library... I have loved the novels of different writers at different times of my life and, during those times, I would read everything from that particular writer... I also read, in the days when it was forbidden, all the Haitian authors whose works had an extraordinary appeal to me, Jacques Stephen Alexis, Marie Vieux Chauvet, Jacques Roumain, etc... I also read the Caribbean classics like Aimé Césaire for example. Two novels, that have both deeply impressed and amazed me, are: *Laissez brûler Laventurcia* by Xavier Orville who is not very well-known and *One Hundred Years of Solitude* by Gabriel García Márquez.

IF: Did you read the Haitian works before or after you departure for Canada?

JD: I read them later. The problem in Haïti is that French literature is taught up to the nineteenth century. Very few Haitian books are available. The other problem is that Haïtian books are traditionally for adults, not for children. I had the good fortune to discover in my family, when I was young, a French literature beyond the nineteenth century. My family had a library schools did not have. The National Library has never been accessible. I enjoyed an advantage schools did not offer.

IF: The narrator of *Memoir* mentions that the little

girl was tired of reading the Comtesse de Ségur's collection, Enyd Blyton's *The Famous Five*; in these passages I could not fail to identify myself with her because, well, these are the same books I read when I was young. I was also surprised to read the same commentaries by Anglophone authors from India and the Caribbean, which means that they too have read the entire collection of *The Famous Five*. That's when I realized that Enyd Blyton was not French but English and that colonialism knows no borders. I wonder whether these books like La Comtesse de Ségur's were also part of your childhood.

JD: Part of all the little girls' in Haiti, all of them! [Laughs] and still nowadays. For example, when I was working in a bookstore, I used to tell people: "you know, there is something else". There is a marvelous literature for children, modern books that are absolutely beautiful!" But no, they would go straight to La Comtesse de Ségur's... When a Caribbean author, male or female, writes a book, like *Haïti chérie* by Maryse Condé, for example, you can try all you want to convince parents that their child will see it's a recent book and on top of that written about his/her country by a well-known novelist; no, it does not work, chances are they will not be convinced.

IF: The same thing happened to me. When I was a young girl, every week, my father would give me five to ten gourdes to buy one or two books at Stella's bookstore or at the Librairie Auguste, because I loved to read. But when he went with me, it was a little bit annoying. He would tell me, "Why don't you go on with La Comtesse de Ségur's collection?" and, if the title was a little risky like *Mon Mari*, for example, by Max du Veuzit, it was not to be touched! Finally, what fascinates me in all this is that it's marvelously placed in the context of feminine conditioning and polishing in Haïti. Thus, I read several years ago the memoirs of Jacqueline Cardozo Turian "*On ne guérit pas de son enfance,*" in it she describes her childhood in Haïti during the 1940s. The title caught my attention because, although it seems to indicate this is the tale of an unhappy childhood, it is that of a very happy, even magical childhood. In your opinion, does one recover from one's childhood? In particular, from a childhood spent like ours under the Duvalier dictatorship or in South American countries where I have noticed many similarities with Haïti for a number of years.

JD: It's very difficult to recover from one's childhood... As for the question of the spoken word, it's a big problem, and I had not considered it in connection with South American dictatorships; this is true and in fact brings us much closer to Latin Americans, because the people from Guadeloupe and Martinique haven't known that, they have known something else.

IF: Exactly, their history is different. We also have a national patrimony, a glorious past if you want, which brings us even a little closer to the South American context and that, at first, however, surprised me.

JD: This is true and I believe that other Haitian writers must also have felt closer to Latin Americans, because when I read García Márquez, his novel *The Autumn of the Patriarch*, I found that the book dealt with things that were familiar to me, more so than Caribbean works do. Historically, Latin Americans are also close to us.

IF: That is interesting, since in the United States, from a geopolitical point of view, Haiti is known as a Caribbean country, "The West Indies" as it is called. Therefore, your explanation of the facts somewhat complicates things but, at the same time, everything becomes more understandable when Haiti is replaced in the context of Latin America.

JD: But on a historical level, it's obvious. At the beginning of the Haitian nation, the solidarity was with Latin America. It is striking, all the same, that Simon Bolivar came to Haiti, that there were Haitians ready to go and fight for the liberation of Latin America, whereas if my memory is right, there was no such movement, such ties with the other Caribbean islands.

IF: This is perhaps an extraordinary coincidence, but I also wanted to mention that several women's novels, including yours, have examined the condition of women under a dictatorial yoke in Latin America and have been published during the eighties, like for instance *The House of the Spirits* by Isabel Allende, (1984), *Por la patria* by Diamela Eltit (1986) and *The Republic of Dreams* by Nelida Piñon in 1987.

JD: I must read those books! All that is very interesting! As far as I know, not much has been written about women under the Haitian dictatorship and even less about children. Besides, in Haitian literature, very few novels have been written from the point of view of children.

IF: If I am not mistaken, the Haitian director, Raoul Peck, made a beautiful movie in which the story is viewed through the eyes of a little girl?

JD: Yes, *The Man by the Shore*. What is really funny is that when the film came out in Port-au-Prince, I told Raoul: "Guess what, it's my story of *Memoir* you are telling!" He said to me: "I haven't yet read *Memoir*, the film is the story of a friend of mine." It's amazing! Our experiences have been similar; people did not talk. That's exactly why it irritates me when people insist that my story of *Memoir* is autobiographical! At the time, it was the autobiographical experience of the whole country!

IF: Let's talk about the second part of *Memoir*, Lili living in Montreal. I have always thought that any and all experiences of exile are really individual. And I think that there is in the novel this anxiety to write the text, this country in abscissa and all that, but that there are also moments of harmony when groups get along, moments of solidarity, of human warmth that are totally different from the first part. There are joyful moments when Lili becomes a woman, secures her financial independence, a voice. A question is crossing my mind. According to you, does exile give back an unquestionable autonomy, a voice [not to say also: opens up a path] that cannot be acquired in one's own country?

JD: In fact, I believe it's what I wanted to show. For someone who has lived under a dictatorship, whatever the reason that pushed this person to exile, two things take place: there is the pain of the exile, but this pain is at the same time accompanied by a sense of liberation. When one leaves a country that is under a dictatorship, one should not lie to oneself, it's not honest to say that there is only the pain, there is also the liberation and the joy. Regarding Haiti, no matter the social class, whether it is someone from a privileged class, or from an underprivileged class, there is also either an economic liberation or an intellectual liberation. Even if he suffers in the United States, the Haitian worker who has left his village, discovers positive things, like being able to eat. We always have a tendency in the Haitian tradition to see in exile the pain alone without admitting there is something else beyond that, and that's what I wanted to show. For Lili, who comes from a privileged class [she has never been hungry or else so little], exile will have been at the same time the discovery of racism that she did not know and the discovery of the spoken word. For the first time, she has the right to speak, she is not afraid her words will be censured; she has the right as a woman to say yes or no, which would not have been the case if she had stayed under the dictatorship. She has the right to learn. That's all I wanted to show for opposition between the first and the second part.

IF: One of the passages of *Memoir* which I also liked very much is this solidarity Lili develops with women during her years of exile in Canada, her *marvel women* as she calls them poetically. Could we talk about these feminist passages in the text?

JD: Well, in Haiti, there was a feminist movement in the 1940s. This movement was crushed by the dictatorship. In those days, these women were already ahead of their time. For instance, there were those who preferred to remain celibate so as not to be oppressed by a husband, lawyers and physicians. We hardly came to know this entire generation of women because the dictatorship prevented its continuity, therefore the possibility for young women to learn from the older ones. All these women, I had the good fortune to meet them, to get to know them under the dictatorship and that was for me a way to reconnect with them. It is true that the Haitian woman is oppressed. In some cases women could not serve as models because they had been silenced by the dictatorship. I wanted to show that exile presented also this aspect: to make the connection, which is to say that a young Haitian woman can rediscover the activism of the older women; an activism we had lost, because between 1957 and 1987 there was no feminist movement in Haiti; such a movement would have been interpreted as revolutionary, that was unthinkable in a time of dictatorship. Therefore, it was important for me to show that the discovery of women was as revolutionary for Lili as the discovery of politics or Marxism because one was as repressed as the other. Traditionally, in Haiti, a novelist must be someone who is interested in social questions, in politics. All these writers, we have known, felt invested with a political and social mission, even the women got caught in it, and there has never been women in this tradition to say: "Fine, as a woman too, I need to speak up and discover the other women, even though dictatorship and education have taught us not to think about social issues." In those days, feminine friendship was a friendship built on superficial things. Women could only become friends if they talked only about dresses, hairdos, not about their condition, not about their situation, not about things they wanted to change. Thus, it was important to show that Lili discovers that women can be friends and that one does not have to be another woman's rival.

IF: Could we elaborate a little on the relationship between Lili and her father, a relationship which seems important to me considering the fact there are very few works in Haitian or Caribbean literature in general that explore this great and often adversarial love between father and daughter as you describe it in *Memoir*?

JD: Well, this adversarial theme was for me a romantic pretext, because, in truth, I had a lighter rapport with my father and, during the first ten years of my childhood, I did not have a father.

IF: Because he was in exile?
JD: He was somewhere else. It is a very strong woman who brought me up during my entire childhood. On a romantic level, it was interesting to show what is in fact the reality for some strong women in Haiti. Because of the patriarchal system, it is the father who has the power and delegates the power. ... That aspect had never been much explored. There is also the fact that in the middle class in Haiti, the father plays an important role, above all in the education of the children, even when he is not there.

IF: Jan, what is currently the role of *tirer contes* (storytelling) in Haitian society?

JD: The tradition of *tirer contes* in Haiti is something that has almost disappeared because mothers, aunts, grandmothers or maids were the depositaries of that memory. What struck me is that even the daily expression of this custom has been wiped out by the dictatorship due to the fact that tales are not told during the day. Traditionally, it is at night, but at night people shut themselves in, so already, there was this constraint, as people did not tell those tales indoors but on the veranda or in the courtyard; a whole tradition which fed Haitian literature and that fear, repression have caused to disappear. Recovering this tradition seems important to me. I remember, from the time I was a young girl, entire evenings when people told tales [often the same tales but we never got tired of listening to them] that influenced me much.

IF: Me too, I loved the tales my mother used to tell me when I was a child. So during your adolescence, in the sixties, the tradition of *tirer contes* almost entirely stopped?

JD: Yes, because the night had become hostile. We had to shut ourselves in, because a certain space of freedom was needed, and as soon as one shuts oneself in, there is an atmosphere of anguish that is no longer favorable to those things, obviously. For it's not just the urbanization and modern lifestyle that led to the disappearance of the tales, but the dictatorship. I imagine that in the countryside it was the same, that people no longer had that night space that allowed this kind of things.

IF: Let's turn to the literary technique of *Memoir.* Some passages in the text are written in italics, like for instance Lili's thoughts.

JD: The text's typography comes from my own inter-pretation of the oral tradition. This way of narrating, it's the whole tradition that speaks, someone who responds. I integrated this whole tradition, thus it had to be like in a tale with storytellers and a leader. When people get together in the evening or at night, there are always storytellers and a leader, a kind of *grande gueule*, that is to say someone who knows more tales or has a strong personality and in fact directs the evening. The italics, that's Lili, the leader, and the tales, the different voices that surround the lit-tle girl growing up. There is nothing post-modernist in this, for me it was something else... In the second part of the novel, it is the character of Lili that is important and not the little stories I felt like writing, because I am first and foremost a storyteller...

IF: So, your style is definitively not as some critics maintain a post-modernist technique?

JD: I wonder whether this label is not connected to the fact that *Memoir* does not belong to the previous categories because one must be either magical realism, or something else. I have the impression that it might be connected to this: labels and categories are a must. I do not see myself as post-modernist. I am inscribed in the Haitian tradition, very, very inscribed, first of all on the level of my imaginary and then on the level of this love I have for tales, for stories. Magical realism, I do not live it the way Jacques Stephen Alexis conceived it or like somebody else. I live it in a different way and I feel myself a stranger to no manifestation of Haitian popular tradition or literature. When, for instance, I decided to publish *Evasion*, I asked two or three people to read the manuscript and one of them told me: "Look, that short story, *Une maison blanche avec des rideaux roses*, that's magical realism." I can tell you in secret that it's a dream.

IF: Because in fact, in the Haïtian tradition, what one dreams is reality.

JD: Indeed yes. Magical Realism? I answered him: "No, it's a story I dreamt and it seemed so beautiful, when I woke up, that I felt like writing it down. There are nightmares I have that I do not write down." [Laughs] These labels, they annoy me, they annoy me in connection with my way of writing. I also believe that not to be able to put me in a category disturbed some critics...

IF: Let's talk about the problem of languages in Haïti. Two languages are being used: French, the language of the administration and education, read and spoken by a minority and Creole which is spoken by the total population and still has difficulty asserting itself on a literary level. The protagonist of *Memoir*, at a certain point in the narrative, bemoans the fact she cannot write in Creole. What's the use to write, she exclaims, "they do not know how to read this language I am using, because I do use it, with difficulty, although I feel it mine neither in my heart nor by right." (52). You also spoke in your text of the anxiety you felt about writing in a tongue which limited you somewhat in your main goal to be read.

JD: Writing in French presents a big problem in so far as I have always had the feeling that Haitian writers were in an absolutely uncomfortable position. There is a contradiction in the situation of a Haitian writer because, what is fascinating in a country with an approximately 70% illiterate population is that there is an incredible number of books being constantly published. So, that's what is fascinating. I have always wondered: how can one be a Haitian writer in a country where the majority of the people cannot read you? There is no chance they'll read you since they can read in neither tongue, neither in French nor in Creole. Now, in the 30% remainder, there are very few people able to read you. They have been alphabetized in a functional way, able to read a legal document or sign their names. They are not readers and that's it, when a thousand copies of a book are published in Haitian, that's the maximum, so that's the big contradiction. There are so many Haitian writers and so few readers! Therefore, regarding the problem of the language, for a long time I have been frustrated, stuck by the fact I could not write in Creole, until one day I told myself that even if I wrote in Creole who would read me? Because whatever the tongue, there are these 70%. I do not have to feel guilty not to write in Creole nor unhappy because, I do not master my mother tongue well enough, to my liking, to be able to write it. In reality, the problem is not a question of tongue, it's that people can neither read nor write in either one of the two languages. One should not even say "If I wrote in Creole, I would be more read!" No, it's not true, those who read Creole literature are those who read French literature because there are very few people alphabetized only in Creole that are able to read Creole literature. The very small percentage of literates have an insufficient command of the language to read a Frankétienne for example, therefore Frankétienne in Creole is read by those who can only read him in French. It's a terrible contradiction! A poet writes in Creole but he is only read by people who can read him in French. It's a terrible schizophrenic situation!

IF: Therefore, it's not really the question that I am betraying my mother tongue, of feeling torn between two languages, it's a lot more complicated than that, no?

JD: Ah yes! What I say is that if you decide to write, you write, period!

IF: And from an economic point of view? What is the response of the Deschamps Editions concerning the publication of Haitian books?

JD: There are no publishing houses in Haiti but rather publishers. The Deschamps Editions are a printing house. This means that authors must themselves pay for the cost of having their books published. All the Haitian writers that live and publish in Haiti are their own publishers. As for me, what I had earned for *Memoir* helped me publish

Evasion and for *Inventer la Célestine* what I had earned for *Evasion*.

IF: Could this possibly change?

JD: That will be very difficult since the market is very small. There is a publishing house in Montreal, called CIDIHCA that publishes books in Haiti. I do not know how much longer they will be able to last; you see, I published *Evasion* without making a profit, and a publishing house cannot do that. So, how can they make a profit? I don't know! It's not possible to sell Haitian books at a higher price, as they will not sell.... Moreover, books are very expensive in Haiti; we receive books mainly from France, therefore if they are not translated in French we will not get them because we have no contact with the Latin Americans, even, Cuban, publishers or distributors. We did not have any contact with Cuba for a long time, now they are starting again.

IF: And yet, a good number of Haitian people speak and read Spanish.

JD: Yes, but they do not sell these books. I discovered Edwige Danticat through someone who told me there was a Haitian female writer who had published a

book in the United States and then, while leafing through a French catalog a little while later, I saw her name. I told myself "Oh, she has also published a book in France." I was not aware that it was the same book published in English – *Breath, Eyes, Memory* under the title of *Le cri de l'oiseau rouge*. I decided I had to order it. If the book had not been translated in French, we would not have
gotten it!

IF: And the books written by the Haitian diaspora, do they reach Haiti?

JD: With great difficulty, through people who enter the country. We have no contact with Canada, either, we are too small a market for them, Haiti does not interest them. For France, it's a question of prestige, France has to be represented in Haiti, therefore books from France get here...

IF: I would like to end this conversation with three questions. Has your outlook on life changed since the murder of your father, i.e. since April 3, 2000? What are your hopes for Haiti's bicentennial, on January first 2004, and what are your plans for the future?

JD: [Long pause] Irline, it's very difficult to answers

those questions. I am quite discouraged by the national situation of this country, the feeling that all the struggles of the past fifteen years are to be fought again. The people we elected show themselves as corrupt as their predecessors. I had no illusions before, but I used to tell myself: we are going to move forward little by little, step by step, very slowly, but resolutely. But each conquest I thought we had won, each development is put again into question. I am living very painful moments presently! It's very depressing to go on fighting the same struggles and get the same results. As for Jean's murder, I must continue to fight, even if in vain! Perhaps one day we will know what happened. What's mostly missing is willpower, and yet people have a great potential. The police enquiry found nothing. Concerning my writing projects, I still cannot bring myself to writing since the assassination. I had started a project, but have been incapable to think about literature lately. Even my cultural, or semi-literary, if you want, program at the Radio is starting to suffer a little. In the end, I have two choices: I leave the country, not on a whim, not because I fear for my life, but because in the long run I find myself absolutely blocked, tied up and no longer functioning, or I stay in my homeland and continue the fight[1].

IF: Thank you Jan for these two interviews, your friendship and your generosity.

Translated by Marie-Josèphe Silver

1 In 2003, Jan Dominique decided to shut down Radio Haiti and return to Montreal where she had lived earlier. "It was becoming almost impossible to do our job. Every time a journalist stepped out, he/she was threatened. It's absurd for a journalist to have to work with a bodyguard."